A Shot in the Dark

A Shot
in the Dark

by David Garnett

LITTLE, BROWN AND COMPANY

Boston/Toronto

PRINTED IN THE UNITED STATES OF AMERICA

To Rosemary Hinchingbrooke

A Shot in the Dark

Chapter I

It was after dark when robert harcourt arrived at san Frediano in the car he had hired at Forlì. They had turned off the Via Emilia and had begun to climb a zigzag road into the hills. Little clusters of golden lights shone down from a great height. At hairpin bends in the road vineyards were lit up in the headlights. The car passed through an arched gateway and he was driven at once to Signor Lucchesi's shop high up the steep main street of the little hill town.

In the light of the open door the pharmacist seemed a good deal older than the American expected. He was a fat little man, wearing a white coat, entirely bald, with big dark eyes magnified by the thick lenses of white-rimmed spectacles and wearing a white hearing aid in the right ear. His greeting was limp, his voice undemonstrative but full of quiet authority as he invited the new arrival to come into his shop. As soon as Robert heard him speak, he remembered

3

that Lucchesi was the mayor of the town and its principal citizen.

"We are waiting for you to eat with us," he said in English. "If you will pay him, I will tell the driver to take your luggage to the lodging I have taken for you at the top of the town." He began giving directions in rapid Italian which Robert could not quite follow. "No need for you to go. It is all-a right," he added as his visitor protested feebly, uneasy at being separated from the cabin trunk, chiefly filled with books, which he had brought with him. Then, taking the big note, Lucchesi went out and gave the driver directions. Left alone, Robert Harcourt looked about him with interest, the entire shop was lined with dark polished chestnut paneling containing drawers and cupboards, each of which was labeled with the Latin name of a drug, inlaid in ebony. Two seventeenth century busts occupied niches in one corner; along the top paneling were jars of beautiful blue ware. All was bare and dignified and there was not an advertisement to be seen. The little man in the white coat suddenly reappeared and handing Harcourt his change, bolted the street door, extinguished the light and led the way upstairs.

The room above the shop, on the first floor, was surprisingly civilized. There were some beautiful North African rugs on a marble floor, a fine piece of Negro sculpture and a vase full of dark clove carnations in the window. A moment later the door opened and a slim dark girl came in and held out her hand to him.

"This is my daughter, Gemma."

Robert must have shown surprise, for the mayor of San Frediano explained, "She was still only a little girl when your friend Major Stephenson brought his sister out to see us, the year after the war."

"Yes, she told me you had a little girl," said Robert, but refrained from adding that Caroline had said she was "all eyes."

"They grow up, you know," said Lucchesi. "It is twelve years now that the war finish."

Robert had never met Patrick Stephenson, and it was Caroline who had told him how the Fascists had come to the shop in the middle of the night and had shot the pharmacist's wife for refusing to tell them where her husband was hidden, but they had either not noticed, or had not bothered about the child lying under the bedclothes. When they had gone she had run out into the winter night, leaving her mother lying dead, and had climbed up out of the town into the mountain, to the cave where her father and Major Stephenson were hiding. Caroline had said the child had arrived, still in her nightgown, covered in mud, barefoot, her arms and legs torn with acacia thorns and that she had sat perfectly still while she told her story and gave her warning, that the father had wept, but that the child had not cried then, or afterwards when her father had swabbed the wounds with dettol and bandaged them.

Now the child who had sat so still in the cave that night was telling Robert to put more cheese in his *minestrone,* and was pouring him out a glass of the San Frediano golden wine.

He would not have known about the woman lying with her head in a pool of blood on the bedroom floor and the child climbing the mountainside, if Caroline had not told him. "Until I went out to San Frediano, Patrick had only told me that il Signor Lucchesi was a widower and had a little girl," said Caroline. "I did not hear the full story until I got there." Robert had guessed that Colonel Stephenson was one of those soldiers who do not talk about what they have seen in war and he liked him all the better for it.

Directly supper was over, the mayor had said he would accompany Signor Harcourt to his lodgings.

"La Signora Salerno will be expecting you. Otherwise I would ask Gemma to play to us. She is a violinist and studied music for two years at Milan."

In the town it was dark; there seemed to be no street lighting. They walked uphill, passed through a narrow alley and crossed a market place to a house standing in the corner of the ancient ramparts.

"You will find a fine view from your window when you

wake up," said Lucchesi. Then, while they waited for his landlady to come to the door, he said, "Gemma will come to take you for a walk and show you San Frediano in the morning, after ten o'clock."

"I have brought your lodger, Signora. Good night." And the little man disappeared into the darkness.

The landlady was noisy. She was anxious to show Robert everything and to explain it all at once, to tell him that he could have another blanket on his bed if he wished, that the switch did not work in the *gabinetto,* but that there was a candle, that her daughter was to have married an American, but that he had been killed in a road accident and that Signor Lucchesi had said nothing about laundry. Robert thanked her profusely, and was complimented on his beautiful Italian, but at last becoming exhausted, shut the door of his room on her and went to bed.

The sunlight was falling through the shutters into the large empty room. When Robert had thrown them open, he found that he was looking down over the precipitous city wall into an olive orchard a hundred and fifty feet below. There were Muscovy ducks and white fowls dotted about in it. A few yards below him there was valerian growing in the masonry of the wall, with butterflies on the last crimson flowerheads.

To the left were the mountains, their steep sides still in

7

shadow. The ploughed lands went right up to where rocks broke out, covered here and there in acacia scrub. Above rose up the almost bare rock. To the right of the mountain were vineyards stretching down to the plains. In one of them vintagers were carrying baskets of grapes to a narrow wagon drawn by two white oxen yoked abreast. The vintage was just starting.

Robert had taken a bath, shaved and breakfasted and had just finished unpacking and arranging his books, when Signora Salerno came in to announce that the Signorina Lucchesi was waiting for him downstairs. On her heels, however, came Gemma herself, very quiet and at her ease, as though there was nothing out of the ordinary in entering a man's bedroom.

"I wanted to see for myself whether you are going to be comfortable," was her only apology for the intrusion.

As his landlady remained talking volubly, Robert asked her to bring them two cups of coffee.

"You have brought very many books with you." And while Gemma was turning them over, Robert was able to take a good look at her. She was bareheaded, with a lovely black mane beautifully groomed and brushed, hanging loose on her shoulders. Rather thick black eyebrows arched over her large eyes; she had a powerful aquiline nose between high cheekbones, a fastidious mouth, painted with dark lipstick against her brown skin. She was not tall, but very slim and high-breasted with a ridiculously small waist, dressed in a very dark blue cotton frock, bare legs with rather thick calves and small feet in sandals.

She was smiling, showing very white teeth.

"Now it is my turn to examine you," she said.

Robert Harcourt blushed to the roots of his hair and he was further embarrassed because Signora Salerno came into the room at that moment with the coffee. When she had departed, leaving the door ajar, Gemma said, "Shall I tell you what I see? An Englishman about six feet tall, strong as a bull, almost old enough to be my father, with gray eyes and a rather embittered expression, but who blushes easily. Something has gone wrong — so he has come to Italy. Have I guessed right?"

Robert laughed, feeling suddenly at ease with her. But as he did not want her to pursue the subject of what had gone wrong, he began to tell her about his life.

"You get high marks. But actually I'm an American citizen, though I have lived practically all my life in Europe."

They drank the coffee and went downstairs into the street while Signora Salerno spied upon them excitedly from the window. For the next two hours Robert felt a delightful sense of well-being arising from the companionship of the girl walking beside him. She questioned him and he was led on to tell her that his mother was English and that when she had divorced his father, she had settled in Ventimiglia and had sent him to school in Switzerland. Then his mother had married again — his stepfather was also an American — and when the war came, after the fall of France, he had gone back for the first time to America.

"I was in the Navy during the last part of the war, but that's enough about me. I want you to show me the town."

Gemma walked quietly beside him, spoke gently, pointing out one building after another: the town hall, the cathedral, the bishop's palace on the highest point of all. Listening to her and looking from the old walls back to the lovely figure beside him, the obsession of the last year was forgotten and Robert was able to enjoy himself seeing the ancient little town. Soon Gemma led him outside the town wall and pointed out the marchese's villa among trees and another equally large villa on a neighboring pinnacle.

"If you have the time to walk there with me, I can show you an old Englishman. But I forget. Although he is a Protestant, he happened to be born in Southern Ireland and that saved him from being molested during the war."

"Has he been living here long?"

"More than thirty years. He is a feature of San Frediano. My father will tell you about him; there is a romance but I do not know all the details."

For some reason Gemma blushed as she said this and Robert wondered what she was keeping back.

They walked out of the town along the white road thick

with dust and pitted with deep potholes. Gemma spoke of the letter her father had received from his old companion-in-arms Major Stephenson.

"He is a colonel now," said Robert.

He felt that he ought to explain that he did not know Patrick, who had written about him to her father because Caroline had said that her brother would be able to find just the right place for him to stay in Italy. But he was reluctant to speak of Caroline to another woman; a fear perhaps that he would betray himself.

"Here is Mr. Bannerman," she said suddenly.

Robert looked up and saw within five yards of him, seated in a wickerwork chair in the open iron gates of the drive leading to the villa, a massive old man with long white hair and a white imperial beard. He was dressed in a white linen suit, which had been newly pressed, with a low starched white collar and a bow tie. His face was brick red and from it eyes as blue as the sea stared with a perfectly blank expression at the distant landscape in front of him. The blue eyes did not turn in their direction, or waver; they simply stared stonily into the distance. Between the short fingers, mottled like raw sausages, was an unlighted cigar. Robert looked at the old man with embarrassment even after Gemma had said, "He is deaf. He often does not pay attention."

As they stood looking at him, the dark figure of a woman whose worn face was still beautiful rose from the shadow of a tree where she had been knitting, and going up to them, began to speak to Gemma in dialect in a very ingratiating tone of voice.

"Allow me to present a new arrival in San Frediano, il Signor Harcourt, la Signora Bannerman."

The introduction appeared to afford the old woman immense gratification; the plaintive expression vanished and her beautiful face, wreathed in smiles, was restored to beauty and dignity as she bowed without shaking hands, asked him to visit her and her husband and assured him that he would always be welcome . . . always welcome, always.

Mr. Bannerman, however, took no part in the proceedings: he maintained his unwinking stare at the slopes planted with olive trees below him and at the distant campagna. After thanking the old woman for her kindness, and promising to call when he had settled in, Robert said good-by and Gemma walked back with him to his lodging.

"Really, I have forgotten the details of his story," she said when he asked her to tell him about the old man. It was clear that there was some mystery.

They walked a little way in silence, then she said, "It is always so strange the kind of women that men will fall in love with. If I were a man the only woman in the world for me would be Major Stephenson's sister. I was still a child when he brought her to visit my father in 1947. But I fell completely in love with her, as girls will, and I suppose I am still a little bit in love with her. I can remember the thrill that ran through my whole body when she stroked my neck and asked me to call her Caroline. And after she had kissed me good night, I lay awake till morning. Can you understand that? Tell me — is Caroline still as beautiful as she was?"

Robert waited for a moment and then replied in a perfectly neutral tone, "Yes, she is a very beautiful woman. But she likes to go through life leaving a trail of broken hearts behind her. And for that reason I do not think that she will ever make anyone happy very long — not even herself."

"Happiness is not everything," said Gemma scornfully.

"Without it love is only a painful form of lunacy," he replied.

"You will never make me believe that."

They were back in the center of the town. Gemma went with him to his room to borrow the copy of Shakespeare's sonnets which he had promised her; then she held out her hand and he pressed her cool fingers, but he did not suggest meeting her again as they parted.

Robert had been told by his doctor not to spend another winter in England. He had chosen to expatriate himself to Italy because he knew the language well and was planning to write a book about Italy. There was also a financial reason: the small income left in trust for him would go twice as far in an Italian town as in London and three times as far as in New York. But his real motive was to be out of Caroline Stephenson's reach. He had been in love with her for two years. He had been happy and unhappy, but at last he could endure no more and was anxious to prove that he wasn't tied to her, but a free agent. Robert had told her of his intention before anyone else and Caroline had thrown herself into furthering the plan with enthusiasm. It fed her sense of power to choose her lover's place of exile and she had made her brother write to his old companion-in-arms, the mayor of San Frediano. In a fortnight it had all been arranged. Caroline's parting with him had been extremely emotional; at the last moment he had had to tear himself out of her arms.

She wanted to keep him among the other dangling scalps.

After Gemma had left his room, Robert took his diary out of his locked suitcase and wrote:

> Compared with Caroline other women seem tasteless and heavy.
>
> Even this charming Italian girl who took me for a walk this morning is earthbound. Caroline treads the earth more lightly and is always irradiated with a strange light. She is as soft as the petal of a rose; hard as a polished flint; ruthless and without compassion; inhuman as the Greek immortals; not to be judged by any human standards. Her movements, her gestures, her minutest actions, her dress — each repeats

in its own way the perfection of her face and body. If I were a blind man I could visualize her in entirety from a touch of her hand; if I were a sculptor I could model her whole body from a foot and an ankle. Yet in spite of, and perhaps even because of, this classical Greek quality her mold and her whole character is so exquisitely English that she seems, in any age perhaps but that of Shakespeare, to be an anachronism. This archaic quality — this Greek or Shakespearian directness is a possible explanation of her ruthlessness. In all her dealings with men and women she seeks not love alone but love and power — power to mold them into the enrichments and ornaments of her personality that her taste demands. For one to worship her divinity is not enough for her; one has to be the right shape to fit into the mosaic pattern of her life. And I — an American — am very far from worshiping any woman as a divinity, or from squeezing myself into a bit of jigsaw puzzle.

And yet she loved me for a whole winter. I possessed her body — but only her body — and she possessed me entirely, body and soul. Then perhaps because I demanded too much, did not fit into her pattern and so no longer interested her, I was cast aside for a Peruvian-Spanish-Indian racing motorist, always half asleep unless his life was in danger — and he in turn for a French actress — for there were always her strange devastating passions for her own sex . . .

Robert shut the book and locked it up in a rage. "I'll be damned if I let her shadow project itself over this little town because she once spent three days here with her heroic brother and made the mayor's daughter fall in love with her!" he exclaimed.

Robert was attracted by Gemma, but he felt that it would be better not to see her if she was going to talk about Caroline: he had come to Italy so that he should never hear her name again. But he would be bound to see Gemma again before long. She would return the book of sonnets and borrow another one and stay to talk about Shakespeare and, no doubt, about Caroline. She probably would compare her to the Dark Lady of the sonnets — and really she would not be much more stupid than he was himself. He must stop minding it when he heard Caroline's name.

Chapter 2

ROBERT WAS ANXIOUS NOT TO INVOLVE HIMSELF IN SOCIAL LIFE and foresaw that he would see quite enough friendly and hospitable Italians if he lived for six months in San Frediano. After all, he had come to Italy in order to be alone and to write his book. Two days went by without interruptions, but then, in the middle of the morning, just as he was settling down to study the relations of Mazzini and Mrs. Carlyle, Signora Salerno bustled in to announce a visitor, the Signor Ercole Beccofilandria. She had told him that the Signore was busy, but he asked when he could come back.

Robert asked her to show him up and immediately a short stout young man wearing spectacles appeared in the doorway and making an exaggerated, insincere bow, announced in English, "If not convenient now, will return in one hour."

"*Buon giorno,*" said Robert.

"Permit to welcome the Signore to our city and to introduce the Thersites of San Frediano."

17

Robert found himself clasping moist stubby fingers, inviting his visitor to have a drink and after an instant of hesitation during which he remembered who Thersites was, he asked, "Why do you describe yourself as Thersites?"

"I am the scurvy knave, and rail against them all: the Trojans and Greeks — the Communists and the Catholics." He took a glass of wine and reverting to Italian, began to explain his position.

"My father is an important figure, the vet. He is brilliant, up to date: injects cows with calcium and calves with penicillin and wants me to succeed him in his profession. But I am antipathetic to animals, probably because I am afraid of them." The eyes twinkled, inviting sympathy. Robert did not doubt the young man's word and was surprised to find himself being amused by his odd visitor.

"So you see I am a misfit. I try one thing and then another. At present I am the town photographer. One day the police will plant some indecent photographs on me — there will be a scandal and I shall have to find a new job."

"Have the police a grudge against you then?"

"Not at all. But I am the scurvy knave. Someone or other is always furious and the others are all laughing. Just now it is the bishop's secretary; I got a snap of him jazzing all alone in the palace when he thought no one was looking, and now it is hanging in the window of the dance hall."

"You must have an amusing life."

18

"Not at all. My tongue, or my tricks are always getting me into trouble. Dull people are much happier. I always regret my jokes . . . What I really enjoy most of all is bird-watching."

"But you scarcely have any birds in Italy," said Robert.

"Little birds. I watch little birds."

"But isn't there anybody whom you admire, or who appreciates you?" asked Robert.

"There's only one man in San Frediano for whom I give a curse. He is a certain Angelo, whom all my father's friends hate and affect to despise. Really they are all a bit afraid of him. He's a strong man and as you know strong men are no longer politically fashionable in Italy. But in another three or four years I'm willing to bet that he'll be mayor and they will all be eating out of his hand. I would like you to meet him."

Robert kept his visitor to lunch and before they parted he had learned that Signor Lucchesi was an atheist but a leading member of the Christian Democrats, that Gemma had been engaged to be married to a ship's officer whose boat was in the Pacific, and that Signora Bannerman had been employed in a brothel in Naples when her husband first met her. Robert wondered just how reliable these bits of information might be.

"You will not find it difficult to acquire a mistress — but the girls here are deadly dull," his visitor said in English as he took his leave. He had obviously kept the remark to the last, but Robert only laughed and waved his hand.

The old Baedeker, dated 1913, which Robert had bought out of a box in Bologna, said:

"San Frediano . . . Duomo dedicated to the Immaculate Conception, is built on the site of the Roman temple of Diana. The Crypt and its foundations date from the 4th century A.D. Adoration of the Magi by Bassano. Frescoes by Mantegna (restored 1883). Bishop's palace designed by Palladio with ceilings and frescoes in the private apartments and chapel by Veronese. Application for admission (to the bishop's secretary) is often refused."

The Romanesque Cathedral was vast and bare and the beauty of the nave for a moment recalled Ely. Under the lantern, and at right angles to the altar, was a more than life-sized figure of the Virgin standing upon a crescent moon of solid silver. She was curiously like Caroline Stephenson. Or was he just a stark, staring monomaniac who was seeing things? The figure was apparently made of wax and dressed in an extraordinary flowered robe of silver spotted with red, over which a veil fell from each side of her forehead. A silver coronet was pressed upon her flowing masses of dark golden-brown hair and she was holding what was obviously a little girl by the hand. It seemed clear to Robert that she was Diana, little changed except in name. He would have examined her more closely if there had not been half a dozen women, most of them young, prostrating themselves before her. Though he was to return many times to the cathedral to make certain that the resemblance to Caroline was real and not imaginary, he never found less than two women worshiping Diana. So the inhabitants of San Frediano, whether consciously or unconsciously, had been worshiping Diana for at least two thousand years and probably for far longer. Did any of them know it? Was there, perhaps, a secret Dianic cult, still in existence in the town, or the neighboring countryside? When he went back to his room Robert took up Seltman's *Twelve Olympians* and read the passage in which Diana was defined not only as the virgin goddess of the chase, but as the protector of all young women in trouble, the goddess to whom women prayed for easy delivery in childbirth and who in all circumstances was the guardian of her sex.

The following afternoon Robert noticed that men were decorating the little town with trellises interwoven with branches of vine, brought from the vineyards in wagons drawn by white oxen after the grapes had been picked. On asking about it, he was told that the Festival of the Grape was to be held the next day, which was Sunday. By evening the little town had been transformed; the branches and foliage of a whole vineyard festooned every wall and arcade, and a big dancing floor had been erected in the piazza and flanked with trellises of vine. All was ready for the fiesta next morning. Then, as the twilight came creeping up the mountains from the darkened plain, and the lights came on in the little town while Robert sat in the crowded café sipping his second glass of the pleasant golden wine, a sudden blare of mechanized music fell stunningly from above upon the whole town. It came from high up — from the piazza by the bishop's palace, which Robert had so far been too indolent to visit.

Presently a movement began towards the steep little street that led to it. Girls began sauntering up towards the noise in strings of four or five, walking abreast, strings which divided at the last moment to let a succession of young men, a few with girls balanced sideways on the pillions of their roaring little Vespa motor scooters, get by. Young men followed in groups, the sexes for the most part keeping separate on the street. Robert finished his glass and then from idle curiosity, joined in the general movement. At the last turn in the steep, arcaded little street, the bishop's palace came in view and Robert saw in letters in neon lights the word: DANCING. Light blazed from all the windows on the first floor; loudspeakers poured out noise from trumpet-shaped amplifiers at the corner of the building and the crowd — the men like dark flies and the girls like colored fluttering moths, swarmed into the vestibule, clicked through a turnstile and mounted the grand flight of marble stairs which led to the immense state dining room of the bishops of San Frediano.

For some time Robert stood apart from the crowd in an empty corner of the little piazzetta unable to understand what he saw. High above the neon lights were the shuttered windows of the bishop's apartments. In one window was a feeble light; all else appeared to be darkness. Below, the canned music of rock and roll blasted out upon the air; the brilliantly lit marble entrance hall was lined with fruit machines and by no means all of the girls swarming in were dressed with the modesty enjoined by the church. For the most part girls and men seemed to belong to the poorest class. Like so much else that he had seen Robert felt that he had come upon a mystery. While he walked down the hill, back to his lodgings, a solitary figure moving against the tide, the bands of linked and laughing youths and girls, often broken apart by overtaking Vespas, were still surging up to fill the dance hall; and the blaring music went on with scarcely any intermission until after midnight.

Next morning the little town was soon full, and while Robert was looking out of the window, a radiant girl dressed in the traditional Italian peasant dress of a hundred years ago burst into the room laughing. It was a moment or two before Robert recognized Gemma, for she was entirely transformed by her full pink and green short skirt and tight-waisted bodice, which pushed up and revealed much of her brown bosom. On her head was a curious flat square of starched cotton.

"Today is the Festival of the Grape. I have kept a seat for you beside my father on the edge of the platform on which we are dancing. We dance all the old dances of the district."

Robert was so surprised that he merely muttered, "Thanks a lot. What time am I to come?"

"Do you like my dress? Do you think I look beautiful? Are you pleased that I should come and seek you out again?"

Robert found himself blushing and said, "Of course I am much flattered. Your dress is certainly lovely."

"Only my dress? Look at it very carefully because the reason I have come is because I want you to write a long letter to Caroline, telling her all about my dress and our old songs and dances."

Robert's face must have betrayed some feeling which Gemma misunderstood, for she drew herself up and looked at him, fierce, astonished and angry.

"I do not want ever to write to Caroline again," said Robert slowly, "but if you wish I will write and tell her what a beautiful woman you have become and how well your dress suits you."

At the pain in his words, Gemma's whole expression changed once more. She looked him full in the eyes for some time, then slowly nodded her head, and murmured, "Forgive my stupidity."

The tenderness of her face and the charming coquetry of Gemma's dress were in such delightful contrast that they effaced the momentary exasperation which the reference to Caroline had called up.

"You are a darling and I like you very much," he said, and suddenly taking her in his arms, he kissed her on the mouth.

She kissed him back and for a brief moment lay in his arms.

Suddenly disengaging herself she said, "Come, we must go at once. The first dance is in half an hour." Then, snatching his hand, Gemma kissed his palm and Robert stroked her on the shoulder as they went downstairs. He felt relieved that he had revealed his secret and that he could be happy in the companionship of this lovely girl who was still so much like a child.

Robert found himself placed on the edge of the dancing floor between Signor Lucchesi, who as the mayor was the most important secular figure present, and the bishop.

Four musicians, a soprano, and a baritone for the solos and to lead the chorus, and five pairs of dancers made up the company. They were all dressed in traditional costume — the men in knee breeches with thick white stockings, open shirts and bolero jackets, the girls in their short full skirts and tight bodices. Their very appearance seemed to infect the whole audience packed in the piazza below with a gay hilarity which reached its height among the singers and dancers themselves.

In the first dance one of the men sat on a chair in the middle of the platform holding a mirror in his hand, and one girl after another stole up behind him and looked over his shoulder. As each face was reflected, the man wiped the mirror vigorously with his handkerchief and made a face of disappointment, or even of disgust, and the rejected girl flounced away pouting with indignation. At last his wished-for partner's face was reflected and the young man sprang up, put down the mirror and danced a *pas de deux* with her. At its conclusion a girl took the place of the man in holding the mirror, and the dance proceeded in reverse, and this was continued until all the dancers were satisfactorily paired off. This was followed by songs, usually with a leader and a chorus and by many square dances, boleros and minuets.

But as they went on, the hilarity of the dancers and the gaiety of the crowd became so great that often the dancers could not act their allotted parts — the girl who was supposed to spurn her adorer scornfully could not keep herself from laughing. Such failures brought delighted cries of humorous encouragement from the crowd. Everyone in the piazza and seated round the platform appeared to be in a state of quite childish enjoyment and all instinctively knew how to strike the right note of frivolous intimacy and good nature. It was a marked contrast to the wolf whistles and salacious guffaws with which a group of youths hanging round the turnstile of the dance hall had greeted some of the girls the previous evening. The complete change of tone could not very well be because of the presence of the bishop, since he had been only a few yards away in an upper story of the palace the night before. He was a lean, brown-faced old man, with a big hooked nose that almost touched his toothless lower jaw, which was underhung like that of a salmon kelt.

In one of the intervals Robert turned to him and asked if he might visit the bishop's apartments in the palace where he had heard that there were ceilings painted by Veronese.

"Come on Tuesday, my son," replied the old man. "And I shall enjoy your visit all the more if you will stop and have luncheon with me."

When at last the dancing was over, the old man rose and spoke gently of the age-long traditions of Italy and of how the feast was held to impress upon them all the love, the goodness and the bounty of God towards all his children. Then the ancient prelate, followed by the notables of the town and the dancers and singers, led the way to the cathedral where a short service was held. But before leaving the piazza, Robert accepted an invitation to dinner that evening from the mayor.

To his surprise he found that it was held in an upstairs room of the principal inn and that there were several other guests. He was introduced to the schoolmaster and his wife, to the doctor, his wife and two daughters, and to the vet and his very pretty young wife, who said as they were intro-

duced, "I am so grateful to you for being kind to Ercole."
After a puzzled moment Robert realized that he was her
stepson. They all seemed to be genial bourgeois figures. With
the exception of Gemma the ladies were dull and kind and
the men anxious to be correct. Though he did not suspect it,
Robert's presence had put a brake on the chaffing and leg-
pulling with which the gentlemen would have shown their
wit. However, if he at first put rather a damper on the company, he later dropped a spark which led to an explosion
of feeling.

They sat down and ate. The food was abundant, richly
and deliciously cooked. There was soup with vegetables,
green noodles made with spinach and served with sweet-
breads and tomatoes, roast kid with rosemary, green peppers,
chocolate meringues, cheese and fruit. Everyone ate enormously and did not scruple to show enjoyment. The red
wine had the faintest trace of fizziness but was drinkable,
which in Robert's opinion was all that can be hoped for
with most Italian wine. As they were eating dessert, the
sound of the canned jazz from the dance hall floated down
from the bishop's palace. For the third or fourth time Robert
was expatiating on how much he had enjoyed the fiesta and
its traditional dances.

"And thanks to our mayor, you were so well placed!
Sitting beside our dear bishop. He is so deeply charmed by

the old traditions and he is so broad-minded!" exclaimed the doctor's wife.

"So one can tell by listening out of the window," said Robert.

"I don't understand," said the lady.

"I mean it is extremely broad-minded of him to allow his palace to be used as a dance hall on Sunday evening," said Robert.

There was an immediate outcry from all the company, except Gemma and her father.

"Listen to that!" "So that is the impression made on visitors!" "The good bishop dragged in the mud." "Signore, I can assure you that the poor bishop is completely helpless in the matter." "He is being driven into his grave by misery and indignation." Such were some of the remarks which burst almost simultaneously from the company.

"Permit me to explain the situation impartially, as I see it," said the schoolmaster pompously. "The use of the diocesan palace as a dance hall is in reality a piece of clever communist propaganda, aimed at discrediting the bishop himself and the authority of the church. Not only is it intended as an insult, but it is designed in order to associate traditional piety with cultural and economic backwardness and communism and atheism with a forward-looking way of life."

"For that reason I regret the bishop's associating himself with the Festival of the Grape," said the vet.

This produced a hubbub of disagreement which Robert found too obscure to follow and which threatened to become so acrimonious that he thought it better to draw attention to himself by asking, "Why cannot the bishop control what goes on in his own palace?"

This drew a chorus of replies.

"It is the fault of his secretary. The bishop and his secretary were deceived by that scoundrel Angelo."

"They should never have signed such a lease."

"They should appeal for the lease to be annulled."

"Let me explain in a few words," said the schoolmaster. "The palace was in a ruinous condition. As the diocese was without funds and the bishop did not wish to appeal to the Minister of Fine Arts, his secretary persuaded him to let off the two lower stories of the palace in return for a handsome premium which has been spent on repairs. The money was paid by a certain Angelo who had returned from America and pretended that it was to be a hostel for tourists. But he has turned it into a dance hall. It is believed that Angelo received the premium as a secret subvention from the Communist Party in order to attack religion and morality. Since its establishment the bishop has lost the sympathy of many young people by the bitterness of his denunciations of jazz music and of modern dancing. That is why he took such a prominent part in the fiesta yesterday. By his unfortunate handling he has allowed the matter to appear as a fight between new and old ways of life and, as so often, the church has allowed itself to be put in an untenable position."

The vet cut in with, "The bishop's secretary says that if he could get the dance hall prohibited, he would allow Angelo to run the rooms as a cinema. By his tactlessness in letting this be known he has made an enemy of the cinema proprietor, who now supports Angelo, who until then was his greatest rival."

At this revelation of ecclesiastical naïveté, there were groans and hoots from the company. Up till then the young ladies had said nothing. Now the doctor's elder daughter, a thin red-haired girl with a pretty face, said quietly, "The preoccupation of the church with women's dress seems to me to play into the hands of its enemies. How can one take seriously these edicts about the lengths of skirts and the cut of bathing dresses which seem to wish to put us back into the out-dated ways of life of our great-grandmothers?"

"I agree with Emilia entirely," said the vet's wife.

"Well, let us hear the younger generation," said the schoolmaster, turning to the younger of the doctor's daughters.

"When I was invited by my cousins to stay at Montecatini, I wore shorts to play tennis and I saw no reason to consult my confessor," said the girl, who was plump, dark and daring, and quite unlike her elder sister.

31

"But you don't wear them in San Frediano," said the schoolmaster.

"No. I don't wear them because we are a small backward community and if I did, it might offend some of my father's elderly patients, which would be bad for his practice."

Everyone laughed with enjoyment at this piece of honesty. "What do you say, Gemma?" asked the younger girl.

"I think the real tragedy is that we cannot create a more harmonious modern world. There is no reason why rock and roll should not be as beautiful as the old traditional dances, or modern painting and sculpture as fine as that of the Florentines. But all our genius goes into science, into medicine and engineering, and while we make these marvelous discoveries the world becomes hideous. But I suppose we must live in the modern world whatever its faults. Do you agree with me?" she asked, turning to Robert.

"Not altogether. I think each of us should choose out of the available possibilities those things in life which matter most to each of us individually. Some of our choices are thousands of years old, others are the most recent discoveries. In Italy you are particularly fortunate: you can live in a lovely seventeenth century palace and have it fitted with modern conveniences. What seems to me tragic is that while so much beauty from the past is preserved in all your lives, the things you have chosen from the modern world are noisy, ugly, trivial and vulgar. The world of tradition is represented by peasants ploughing with yokes of white oxen between lines of grapes growing uneconomically but prettily on fruit trees — the new world by hideous advertisements every hundred meters along the highway, and motor scooters that make fifty times as much noise as an American car."

Robert's criticism was instantly refuted by a chorus from most of the company present, and he was reminded that Italy was in the forefront of modern progress and that a certain price had to be paid for modernism.

"In spite of which," said the schoolmaster with magisterial huffiness, "the Santa Trinitá Bridge in Florence, blown up by the Germans, has recently been rebuilt out of the very stones of the old bridge, or from stone taken from the same quarry as the original bridge. What other country would have done the same? And the Santa Trinitá Bridge is not the only one. The Bridge of the Scaligers at Verona was rebuilt immediately after the war and it is now indistinguishable from the original. Yet the Italian workmen who made these copies, also lead the world in the construction of mountain roads and modern bridges as you will admit if you ever drive over the Appenines from Forlì to Florence."

Anxious to make amends for his lapse, Robert began to praise everything Italian, and harmony was completely restored before the company separated. The little town was still drenched in the American dance records disseminated from the bishop's palace.

Chapter 3

ROBERT'S NAME WAS CALLED IN TONES OF EAGER EXCITEMENT
as he passed the café in the piazza, and he saw Ercole
Beccofilandria sitting at a table with a man he did not know.
Robert walked up, and the man, without rising from his seat,
or taking the cigar out of his mouth said in English, "Meet
Tommy Angelo."

He was a strikingly handsome man of about forty, with a
mass of gold-brown hair brushed straight back from his
forehead, eyes the color of bruised green olives and a frank
open smile which showed a perfect set of even white teeth.
Robert leaned forward to shake hands with him and accepted a whisky sour which he offered.

"How long you reckon to stay in San Freddy?" Angelo
asked him.

"Till I've finished writing my book."

"Meaning?"

34

"I haven't any idea. Perhaps a year, or more."

"How come you pick on this little burg?"

"A friend of mine told me about it."

"Like it?"

"Yes. Don't you?"

"Suits me fine."

"You run the dance hall, don't you?"

"Yup."

"It seems pretty popular."

"I like-a people 'appy. We Italianos like people 'appy. We are naturally 'appy people. Love music and dancing. The people work verra 'ard all the week. They want fon and 'appiness on Saturday night and Sunday and I give it them. I like-a to see the girls and the boys 'appy together. You hear it, Saturday, Sunday night?"

"I certainly do."

"It is a lovely music — what we call *'un bel rumore,'* a swell noise — and I give it to all the town free of expense. They all like it."

"The old bishop doesn't like it much, does he?"

"I have kept a roof over the old man's head. No, the bishop is fine old fella. I have had some complaints from a few moldy old peanuts belly-aching about the boys and girls dancing. I guess a few of them would like to run me out of town. But they will learn what is good for them. I want everyone to be 'appy; all San Freddy to be one big family.

I want the Communists and the Catholics to dance all their trouble away."

"You'll have to convert the bishop to liking rock and roll as much as he likes the old traditional dances."

Angelo laughed good-humoredly.

"Show our egghead friend your snap of Mangoni — that's the bishop's secretary."

Ercole took a photograph out of his wallet and passed it to Robert, who laughed as he saw the young priest holding up his cassock in one hand as he executed a high kick.

"I got two or three amusing ones at the fiesta yesterday," said Ercole. "Here's a rewarding one of the bishop."

It was a close-up showing the nutcracker profile peering at the corsage of one of the girls dancing. But when Ercole passed it to Angelo the latter shook his head.

"No do," he remarked. "What I want is the old guy looking at a broad in a bikini."

Robert would have been willing to lounge away an hour gossiping with Ercole and looking over the photographs, which he was anxious to show. But it was obvious that Angelo wanted him to go. It seemed odd to Robert that this should be so, but he felt sure that the proprietor of the dance hall regarded him with suspicion. He got up to go, but Angelo lounged forward and said:

"I'll be real glad if you'll date up the Signorina Gemma for Saturday night and bring her up my place."

36

"Quite an idea," replied Robert.

"Well, I'll be seeing you then," said Angelo.

Robert Harcourt walked away with his fists clenched with anger, uncertain whether the man had meant to be offensive or not. But the odd thing was that in spite of the last piece of damnable impertinence, he was surprised to find he rather liked the fellow.

It was the bishop's secretary, Father Mangoni, who received Robert Harcourt when he had climbed the flights of marble staircase and had been shown into an immense empty waiting room, paneled in walnut sculptured with the arms of a forgotten cardinal. Mangoni was a very dark, lean and active little man with a chin so blue that he always seemed in need of a shave and a skin so greenish brown that he always seemed in need of soap and water. His dark black eyes shone perpetually with an eager faith and Robert felt certain that Father Mangoni could never see either a joke at his own expense, or two sides to a question.

These observations were made as Robert followed his guide round the great rooms of the palace, looking at the Veronese ceilings, which were magnificent, and the frescoes in the bishop's bedroom, which showed Diana hunting with a band of lightly draped female companions, hounds leaping through a forest and pulling down a stag.

"The cathedral is built upon the site of a Roman Temple to Diana and I seem to have detected the vestiges of a cult of the goddess in the town. Do you think that these frescoes are in any way connected with it?" asked Robert. But Father Mangoni did not seem even to understand his question — he merely shrugged his shoulders and said:

"There is always a great deal of artistic license in mural decoration . . . The paintings are those of the sixteenth century."

"Yes, of course," said Robert impatiently, "but I wondered whether you had ever become aware of a streak of paganism in this district, especially among the women?"

Mangoni's eye flashed, his blue-black, badly shaven upper lip curled back in a snarl, revealing very white teeth marked with jet black stains between them. "Pagan? — I would say they are given over to diabolism and to unnatural vice. The women attend mass, they pray — but of what nature are their prayers? Immodest, lewd, untruthful, nine out of ten girls in this town are instruments of Satan. Even when the fires of the flesh have expired, the old women are far more unchristian than the men."

Robert had been wondering whether the frescoes of the goddess indicated that the sixteenth century bishop for whom they had been painted had been an adherent of the Dianic cult described by Dr. Margaret Murray. If so the present division of the palace into Christian and pagan halves was nothing new. But it was evident that such a cult was anathema to Father Mangoni, and Robert judged that there was nothing to be gained by questioning him further on the subject.

"I didn't see you at the Festival of the Grape," said Robert. "Don't you care for the old traditional things?"

Mangoni seemed annoyed. Finally he said:

"All these things are very interesting for you, because you are a foreigner. But they are not important to us. We have to live in the modern world — to guide the children of today in the era of atomic power. We must learn to think in terms of modern instruments: television, cinema, radio, to be ready for new ways of life and new values, and not to let our people be corrupted by them." The black eyes were burning with intensity, he was about to say something more, but at that moment the door opened and the old bishop entered.

His brown nutcracker jaws creased into smiles as he greeted Robert, then he put his hand on his shoulder and said, "It is very good of a young man like you to come to see an old man like me." When Robert looked round he saw Father Mangoni had left them and the bishop was saying, "You must be tired after looking at all those pictures. Come and have a glass of Marsala — and I think luncheon is ready."

They had the meal together alone and Robert wondered whether Mangoni's anger might not have been because he had not been invited to share it. For most of the meal Robert found himself answering questions about his own life and upbringing. Then when the dishes had been cleared away and the coffee brought in, he cautiously raised the subject of Diana.

"I am interested in the way in which aspects of pagan religion survive locally even till this day: some fountain, sacred to a nymph becomes a holy well associated with a female saint. And it has struck me that the madonna in your cathedral is worshiped in an aspect widely different from the madonna in a French cathedral, such as Chartres. There she is the Queen of Heaven who has almost displaced both Father and Son; here she is particularly the guardian of women in their troubles and is but little concerned with the affairs of men. She is just what Diana was before her, and I am told that your cathedral was built on the site of a Roman temple of Diana."

The lean brown jaws creased in a smile and the eyes twinkled naughtily.

"And why not? We still have a certain tenderness for Diana in this town. She even beautifies the palace walls, as you have seen for yourself. I would say that after conversion and being received into the true faith, the heathen worshiper of a virgin goddess might legitimately worship those aspects of the Blessed Virgin which appealed most to his heart. Diana was a virgin — but not a mother. It would be natural for him to worship the virginity of the Blessed Virgin rather than her maternity."

40

"Diana was the moon goddess and the madonna in your cathedral is standing upon the upturned moon," said Robert.

"Naturally. The immaculate conception, symbolized by the upturned crescent moon, aroused a deeper emotion in the convert because the crescent moon was already traditionally associated with the virgin goddess Diana. I can see nothing wrong in this. We have shifted the crescent from the Virgin's head to her feet. Perhaps it was providentially ordained that the Romans should worship a virgin in order to facilitate the establishment of the True Faith in Italy."

"You put it very well and quite delightfully," said Robert, enchanted to find an attitude so unlike that of Father Mangoni.

The bishop hesitated and then suddenly said:

"I might go further and suggest — though probably heretically — that the worship of certain pagan deities was less revolting to God than that of others. For example, that the worship of the virgin Diana and of Zeus the earth-shaker was less abominable than the worship of Baal and Moloch."

"So you are tolerant of any vestiges of a Dianic cult which may remain?" asked Robert.

"No man can escape error, except the Holy Father," and the bishop crossed himself quickly. "But it is perhaps less offensive to God if we err by reverencing the errors of the past than if we seek out and fly into errors of our own making. If I am right in this, I would say that a Dianic cult would be less offensive to the church than the irreligion of to-day. But there is no such cult here."

"I am glad to find you are so much more tolerant than Father Mangoni," said Robert.

The old man gave a shy, pinched smile.

"I keep him with me to correct a certain laxity to which I am liable, as you may have noticed. I think it arose when I was a missionary in Africa. There I found that my work as spiritual father was to coax the indigenous forms of worship into channels which were acceptable to God."

Robert laughed and looked with affection into the old man's merry eyes.

"Now, my young friend. I asked you to lunch because I have something to ask you of greater urgency than the worship of Diana. Have you been to the dancing down-stairs?"

"No. But I met Signor Angelo yesterday at the café for a few minutes."

There was a silence. The bishop was pressing his hands together, his lips moved soundlessly and he hesitated. At last he said, "My son, if you love Italy, if you love the old simple life of its people, with their pure hearts, if you love the classics, I ask you to help me . . . to help me to prevent this corruption from spreading in the town."

"You know that I am not a Catholic, my lord?" said Robert.

"I know that. But you are not a Communist either. I am not asking help for the church alone, but for the people — to prevent the corruption of their way of life."

"The ways of life must change even in Italy. We have to use the tools that science puts in our hands," replied Robert gently.

"I know that. That is not the question — I am thinking of the ruin of Italy, of the enslavement of our people, of Russia waiting, of the fate of Hungary, of the labor camps into which every honest man is herded. That is the fate which I foresee awaiting us."

"Do you know that Angelo is a Communist?" asked Robert.

"I know that he is an unscrupulous ambitious man. He is ready to serve the Communists, to make use of them and to be made use of by them. He will let nothing stand in the way of his ambition and he can only obtain power through them, by carrying out their plans."

"How can I, a foreigner, who knows nothing of Italian politics, play any part in this?"

"It is just because you are a foreigner that you can help. You can mix with people without suspicion. You can go to the dance hall; you can win the confidence of everyone. I ask you to find out what is happening — to penetrate Angelo's designs which are still obscure to me. Then come to see me again and tell them to me *alone*."

"But I see nothing wrong in the dance hall. I see nothing wrong in young people dancing to American music or in their going to bed together. I do not believe in sin," exclaimed Robert almost angrily. "I am probably more in agreement with Angelo about such subjects than with you."

To his surprise the bishop showed no sign of being shocked but nodded his head with patient understanding.

"I am not talking to you about the weaknesses of the flesh. I am asking you to think of the Hungarian people — of the fate of their writers and scholars and of all honest men. I am asking you to help save Italy from that."

"Well. I will find out what I can. And if I think that you are right in your suspicions, I will help you if it's possible."

The old man was visibly moved. He bowed his head, murmured something to himself, then stretched his hand out and laid it on Robert's head. The old lean fingers gripped the scalp.

"I trust you, my son. And what I have said remains a secret between us two alone." He held out his hand and Robert realizing what was expected, lifted it to kiss the episcopal ring, but before he could do so, the bishop had turned his hand palm upwards and the kiss fell on the underside of the fingers.

Robert felt as he left the palace that he had been enlisted as a secret agent in a war in the existence of which he did not altogether believe. However, he would see what he could do.

His first thought was to fall in with Angelo's suggestion and ask Gemma to go with him to the dance hall on Saturday night and see what she would say. If he were to do that he must see Gemma at once.

"You will find her upstairs," said her father, who was taking down the shutters of his shop after the siesta. Gemma opened her eyes wide when she saw him.

" 'Let not my love be called idolatry,' " she quoted, speaking English with difficulty. "Have you brought me another volume of English poetry? I am steeped in Shakespeare's sonnets and cannot imagine that I shall ever want anything else."

"No. I have come to ask you to come to the dance hall with me on Saturday night."

Gemma looked astonished. "Why?" she asked.

"Don't you like dancing?"

"Do you know what you are asking me to do?"

"Shock your father's friends, I suppose."

"They will not think I am your mistress, because they will say that you are a foreigner and could not be expected to realize that you are compromising a young girl. But, if I accept, they will say that I would like to be your mistress and that I am ready to flout all the conventions."

"Are your friends such horribly malicious people?"

"No. They are not like the only friend you seem to have

made for yourself in San Frediano. I mean Signor Ercole Beccofilandria."

"Do you dislike him?"

"I loathe him. He is the most unpleasant creature I have ever met. Why have you made a friend of him?"

"He amuses me."

"You have no right to be amused, or to encourage such a toad."

"I think he is a truthful toad. And anyhow I'm not responsible."

"Yes you are."

"I'm an outsider. I'm a spectator. I'm not an Italian. Why should I adopt a moral line about the poor young man?"

"You are a human being. Even if you are not an Italian, you must help us to preserve standards of honor and honesty and decency."

Gemma was saying what Robert had heard only half an hour before from the bishop. He looked sulkily at the floor, frowning. "I don't know what you accuse him of doing. But apart from Ercole — leaving him on one side — I suppose that you are right. I came here to escape from everything. But even though I may not share your views about honesty and decency, I admit I cannot abandon my own, just because I am living in a foreign country."

"That is all I am asking you," said Gemma in a half-suffocated voice.

Robert raised his eyes and saw that Gemma had turned away while they were speaking and was looking out of the window. It occurred to him that what she had been saying mattered to her intensely, that perhaps she was hiding her emotion. Yes, she was hiding tears. A sudden surge of tenderness and desire came over Robert; his heart began beating painfully fast and he could not trust himself to speak. He took a step towards her and put his hand on her shoulder. Gemma turned her head towards him and in the next moment she was locked in his embrace and their mouths had met in a kiss.

"All right. I'll come if I can," she said at last when she had released herself. "Go away now. I'll talk to my father about it all."

"We can't part like this. I must know what he says. I must see you again tonight."

Gemma, who had interrupted his words with kisses, laughed and said, "You are very pressing all of a sudden."

Robert stroked her breast and she looked at him with round dark eyes, wild and frightened perhaps by her own feelings.

Robert and Gemma paid their one hundred and fifty lire and clicked through the turnstile unnoticed, and it was not until the music stopped after the third dance that Angelo, wearing a double-breasted, draped dinner jacket, walked up and greeted them.

"Come and have a drink on the house in my office. I got a proposition to make the signorina."

The room was on the ground floor and had heavily barred windows and was furnished with a big safe, a refrigerator, a cocktail cabinet and an electric air-conditioning plant. On an aluminum and plastic couch of the type known as "The Hollywood Dream" lay a fat woman of fifty, whose pale fleshy face, abundant colorless hair piled on the top of her head and a pale-green and straw-colored frock gave her the appearance of a plateful of boiled cabbage. She was smoking a powerful toscana cigar and reading a small book, and wearing spectacles. For a moment or two after their entry, her face was completely indifferent, almost without expression; then, taking off her glasses she was able to see that Angelo was not alone and sat up, thrusting the book behind a cushion. But Robert, who had good eyesight, had already noticed that it was printed in Russian.

"Here are the Signorina Lucchesi and Mr. Harcourt," said Angelo in Italian, and added for Robert's benefit in English, "meet Mrs. Angelo."

The woman almost ignored him, but her manner to Gemma was affectionate. Angelo produced glasses and a bottle of Asti Spumante from the refrigerator. When it came to his wife's turn he paused and she shook her head. She was drinking *grappa*.

"You have studied classical music, Signorina," said Angelo, "and I want you to help me. My wife here, and I, are planning to give some concerts and I want you to choose a swell program of high-fi records. We won't have the outside amplifiers on. People who want to listen will have to come up and buy tickets for the salone. I want you to take on choosing the records, tuning the machine, testing the acoustics of the hall and arranging the seating. I would pay you twenty-five per cent of the takings. What you say?" And Angelo turned to Robert as though expecting him to answer.

Robert hesitated. Then he said, "I would suggest that a San Frediano Musical Society be formed, which would pay you for the use of the hall and should organize the concerts. Signorina Lucchesi should be the secretary."

"My! That's a swell notion. You've got something there — so long as the performances aren't exclusive. I want all the peoples who love the music to come."

"Of course. And I suppose there ought to be all sorts of people in the Society. The difficulty might be to get them to join before the first concert. Once that is a success they'll all want to join. But can we get them to come and make the first concert a success?"

Angelo was watching Robert keenly with his curious, discolored green-olive eyes. Then his face broke into a smile and he showed all his teeth.

"Leave that to me — everyone in the town will come. Only we are not quite ready — the first concert will not be for a month. So I give you a good notice. I want you to get what is first rate, what people can't hear easily anywhere else. Then I'll put it over big. Later on, perhaps we get a big name pianist to come and give a recital . . ."

Gemma and Robert stayed talking about the plan for an hour, the bottle was finished and they rose to go. Mrs. Angelo got out of the Hollywood Dream and kissed Gemma, and they went out. Robert looked at his wrist watch.

"Signora Salerno won't be asleep for another three quarters of an hour. Shall we dance or go out into the country?"

"Let's get away from here," said Gemma.

That night, lying beside each other on a haycock of sweet-smelling lucerne, Gemma concocted a plan by which they could turn Angelo's suggestion of the concert to their advantage. It was clear that she would have to go to Florence to hunt up the recordings necessary for Angelo's concert. If Robert went off saying he was going to spend a week in Bologna, she would go to Florence two days later where he could meet her; they could spend two or three days together in Florence and afterwards return separately.

The little town was full of scandalmongers, their visit

together to the dance hall would excite a good deal of comment and it would be better if they were not seen together again in San Frediano until she had had an opportunity to talk to her father.

"Do you feel excited at spending three days in Florence with me?" she asked as she stood up in the little hayfield and began brushing the dried lucerne leaflets out of her mane of hair.

"Let me brush it," said Robert, but every little while he stopped to kiss her ear, or the nape of her neck and thus it was some time before the last tell-tale bit of lucerne was got rid of.

"Good-by till Wednesday in Florence."

"Good night, my lover."

Chapter 4

IN SOME ITALIAN TOWNS THE WEEKLY PARADE OF FASHION IS IN the evening, but in San Frediano it was during the hour before lunch on Sunday, when the good bourgeois, in his best clothes, strolled with his wife and daughters round the piazza or stopped on the battlements to gossip with a group of friends and neighbors and gaze at the plain below. Robert came back from his solitary morning walk at the fashionable hour and as he crossed the piazza on his way to Signora Salerno's, he was suddenly made aware that he had incurred the displeasure of the respectable families whom he had met at luncheon the week before. As he passed along the battlements, he saw before him the doctor's wife and daughters standing talking to the schoolmaster. Robert smiled and his hand went to his hat, a greeting was on his lips, but there was no answering smile of recognition. Instead of the greeting he expected, he found himself being stared at with a mixture of insolence and curiosity by the schoolmaster and the elder ladies; the two girls kept their eyes on the ground. Robert saw that he was being "cut" and the obvious explanation was that his visit with Gemma to the dance hall the previous evening had become known.

As Robert lunched alone in his room, he wondered how the respectable would visit their displeasure on Gemma. She was strong-minded, but they could strike at her through her father. And though the little pharmacist must be made of strong stuff, he had been ailing for some time. Indeed Gemma had been doubtful up to the last minute whether her father would feel up to going on the day-long excursion to visit Cesenatico with her that he had planned, for that Sunday. When the hour of the siesta arrived, Robert was feeling too restless and uneasy to sleep, or to read. Instead he paced about his room and looked out of the window. Presently he lifted his eyes from the empty piazza to the campanile and caught sight of a movement in one of the three slits in its side. Robert had exceptionally good sight and he was certain that whatever had moved was a man and not a pigeon. He felt sure that there was someone hidden in the embrasure. Perhaps the man was watching him. Robert almost closed the shutters of his window, but left an aperture through which he could watch unseen. After five minutes he saw a head move slightly and there was the flash of the sun on glass or metal. Who could the fellow be? What was he doing up there? And Robert felt a sudden access of Anglo-

Saxon rage at the thought that he was being spied upon in his room — where Gemma might have joined him if it had not been a Sunday when her father had taken her for an excursion.

Keeping close to the wall so as to remain invisible, Robert left his room and ran downstairs, left by the back entrance and walked round behind the duomo to the far side of the campanile. The door, usually locked, was ajar; Robert slipped inside and pushed it to behind him. Then he began walking very slowly up the winding stone staircase. It occurred to him that if it came to blows the watcher standing above him would have a big advantage. But when he had climbed some twenty feet, the bells above broke into furious peals. The noise was almost stunning, but Robert climbed on, realizing that his approach could not be heard. There was the wooden floor just above him and as his head rose above its edge he saw Ercole Beccofilandria hunched up in one of the embrasures with his eyes glued to a pair of field glasses. Robert remembered what the young man had said about bird-watching — but what kind of bird was he watching now? From the direction he guessed that his glasses were riveted on the bedroom windows of the doctor's house opposite and only very slightly below him. Ercole's expensive camera with its big telephoto lens was resting on the floor beside him. This was what the rascal had meant by "bird-watching." And suddenly the real explanation of the "bird-watcher's" relation with Angelo flashed upon Robert's mind. Ercole was Angelo's spy, gathering information about the private lives of the inhabitants of the little town — if possible, backed up by photographs of them in compromising situations. What a skunk the little man was! Gemma was absolutely right about him.

The peal of bells in the campanile was slowing and Robert withdrew unseen before they should end. By the time the last echo of the chimes was over he was back in his room, and looking out of his window he could just catch sight of the shadow of Ercole's profile on the inner side of the embrasure.

Nothing could be gained from an immediate showdown with the snooper. He could not prove that he was watching one of the doctor's daughters, or his wife. For all Robert could prove, there might be a bullfinch in the doctor's garden.

But at least he was warned, and if he kept a good lookout he might be better able to defeat the plans that the old bishop believed that Angelo was hatching.

Next morning Robert followed the road along which Gemma had taken him on their first walk together.

The tall iron gate at the entrance of Mr. Bannerman's villa was locked and on each side the garden was protected by extraordinarily efficient barbed-wire fences. Inside the gate was the cane chair, empty, with a Vespa parked beside it. As Robert hesitated, wondering if he should pull the chain of the bell, two figures came down the path towards him. They were Father Mangoni and Signora Bannerman, and they seemed a good deal surprised to see him waiting outside the gate. However, when the signora had unlocked it the bishop's secretary greeted Robert and shook hands before he wheeled out his Vespa, wrapped his cassock carefully between his knees and started off along the road with a roar. Signora Bannerman seemed to have been favorably impressed by Father Mangoni's having shaken hands with him.

"He is a very holy man. He has brought me to a state of true penitence," she said. "I am very glad that you are honored with his friendship."

She locked the gate carefully after letting him in.

"We have to lock the place," she said. "It is my husband's orders because of the thieves. He will be glad to see you today."

Robert thought that this was unlikely; however, when he had been ushered into the presence of the deaf old man, he found that he was mistaken.

"They told me you were staying in the town and I was hoping to see you," he said. "Do you drink whisky? I've some genuine Highland Park Pure Malt — It's the Orkney whisky and a bit of a rarity . . ." Though it was early for a drink, Robert accepted the stiff tumbler which was poured out for him. He filled up his glass with cold water and they drank.

It was the best whisky that Robert had ever tasted and he shouted the information at the old man, whose manner to him changed completely. As the morning went on, it ripened from ordinary friendship to affectionate complicity. Mr. Bannerman did the talking.

"You wouldn't believe the way these damned priests get hold of the women. I married Emma thirty-five years ago. For thirty years she never went to mass and no priest ever came near the place. Now this ugly black jackdaw would be in and out of the house every day, unless I had forbidden him to set foot in it. So they meet in the garden and go clack-clack, clack-clack — just like jackdaw talk. Emma sneaks off to mass before I'm awake, spends her time telling beads on a rosary. Makes me think I must have married a nun!"

The old man finished his glass of whisky, tasting every drop, and poured out a new glass for himself and filled up Robert's with a shaky hand.

"Did you see the jackdaw as you came in?"

Robert shouted that he had — and then added that he had met him before and didn't much like him.

"But the bishop is a fine old bird," he yelled in order to salve his conscience.

"I've no use for any papists. To hell with the Pope!" replied Mr. Bannerman, and then began coughing violently. His wife, who must have been listening outside the door, hurried into the room and offered her husband a bottle of smelling salts while she patted his shoulder and then wiped the sweat off his neck and forehead with a clean handkerchief.

"You wouldn't believe that that woman would do anything in the world to get hold of my money, would you?" said Mr. Bannerman, when his paroxysm of coughing was over. It was a moment before Robert remembered that she did not understand English, but the remark seemed brutal.

"No, I wouldn't," Robert shouted almost angrily, and the tone of his voice must have been understood.

"I beg you, Signore, not to contradict anything he says. It excites him and is dangerous," said the Signora in Italian, speaking in a low voice so as not to be overheard.

"You wouldn't believe the life I've led with this woman for the last thirty-five years," said Mr. Bannerman in a comfortably reminiscent tone. He seemed positively jolly as he recalled it and Robert wondered what obscene revelations might not be coming.

"My wife's relations have lived on what I give them ever since I settled down here. They've given up working years ago. At first they were in and out of the house all day long. I had to stop that because of the fleas. And of course they were stealing everything they could lay their hands on. So I put up the fence to keep 'em out. Since then there has been one large-scale attempt to murder me, one attempt at a fatal accident, and one poisoning."

"You don't say so!" yelled Robert. Signora Bannerman stood looking at her husband inscrutably.

"He'll be all right now. A bit of talking before his food will do him good. He'll enjoy a good siesta. But please don't excite him," she said, still speaking in a low voice.

"That woman loves me like a dog," said Mr. Bannerman forcefully. "But twenty-five years ago she got up in the middle of the night, leaving me asleep in the bed, went downstairs and unlocked the gate for her three brothers, who had come to assassinate me as I lay asleep. Luckily for me I had got an idea of what was in the wind and had told the *carabinieri* who were in ambush and they challenged them.

"The eldest brother fired at them and they shot him dead. The others ran into the house. But the shooting had woken me up and I took them in the rear with my revolver while the *carabinieri* fired at them through the windows. It was quite a party I can tell you, while it lasted."

"Good God. And you mean to say you went on living here . . ." shouted Robert.

"Emma's two brothers got five years in jail. Of course I forgave her. Told her I would let bygones be bygones. Her brothers knuckled under when they came out and I thought

I was safe. Five years later, damned if her youngest brother didn't push me and the mule I was riding over a cliff . . . I tell you, I've learned that you can't trust these mountain people in the Romagna. For fifteen years I kept a loaded pistol within reach every moment of the twenty-four hours."

"Astounding," bellowed Robert.

Mr. Bannerman nodded and sipped his whisky reflectively.

"That's the word for it. Astounding. I still love her and she loves me like a dog. But if Master Jackdaw put her up to it, she would poison me tomorrow."

"Why on earth should he?" yelled Robert.

"She would like to give all my money to the church to pay for masses for the repose of her soul." Mr. Bannerman chuckled pleasantly. "She doesn't worry about my being stuck in purgatory for half eternity. She tried to poison me once, but I don't think she'll try again."

"Have you any proof of that?" shouted Robert. Mr. Bannerman's revelations were straining his powers of belief.

"You ask your friend Lucchesi. He's a good fellow, by the way. Got more grit than anyone in this town. Emma tried to buy some cyanide from him — said it was to take wasps' nests, but he smelled a rat and sold her soda instead, dipped in bitter almonds to make it smell."

"Why did he suspect her?"

"It was the middle of winter. No wasps. Silly woman didn't think of that. I was very poorly at the time and she served me up a plateful of soup that tasted of washing soda. Directly I tasted it, I said to her, 'This is poison. You are trying to murder me. I shall have it analyzed and send you to prison for the rest of your life.' " Mr. Bannerman paused dramatically and refilled both glasses with whisky.

"She confessed everything and begged for mercy. So I told her: 'Let bygones be bygones.' But you see I lead a funny life here."

"It can't be easy to forgive your wife if she tries to poison you," said Robert, who found his host's readiness to let bygones be bygones the most incredible part of the story.

There was a silence and Bannerman sipped his whisky solemnly.

"Well, what else was I to do? You can't send the woman you've loved for the whole of your life to jail. At least I couldn't."

The would-be poisoner came in and announced that luncheon was ready. Robert refused an invitation to share it and left after promising to drop in any morning when he felt like having a whisky. The woman accompanied him silently to the gate. As she unlocked it and let him out she said, "It will do my husband so much good to see you and talk English. Come again soon."

Mr. Bannerman's story made an extraordinary impression upon Robert Harcourt. His relations with Caroline Stephenson had made him think of any woman he loved as an enemy to be defeated, with whom all was fair, there being no rules in love or war. Her cruelty had engendered in him, as it often does, the philosophy of the rake. His recent success with Gemma had left him astonished, but his attitude had remained unchanged. He loved her body; he loved her company; he was perhaps more than a little in love with her — but it had not occurred to him that his relationship with her might determine the course of his life, or that love once given might not easily be withdrawn.

But when the fiery-faced old Irish Protestant, sodden with whisky, had asked what could he do but forgive the woman who had tried to poison him, Robert's first amazement gave place slowly to feelings of pity and admiration. His emotion was not simply for the Italian prostitute nor for the man who had rescued her. It was more generalized into a sense of the tragedy of a creature who could wish to poison the partner of thirty years and the admiration of the human heart which could forgive, could "let bygones be bygones," and without forgetting, go on living in close dependence on the woman who had sought his death. And far from nursing resentment the old drunkard could see clearly that she "loved him like a dog." And her love was equally obvious in the way she waited upon him and in the voice in which she had warned Robert not to excite him by contradiction. The more he reflected on the story he had heard that morning, the more Robert Harcourt realized that though he was himself more intelligent, better educated, more attractive and more gifted, he was, in what was perhaps the most important human quality of all, Mr. Bannerman's inferior. He had less capacity for love. "Or is it just that I'm not so courageous? That old chap is a hell of a brave man!" But possibly the qualities of love and of courage went together. Robert had no doubts about the story, but he would have liked to have gone at once to Lucchesi to hear his version of the attempt at poisoning. But he had not seen Gemma's father since he had taken her to the dance hall and was afraid that he might make a scene which would embarrass his relationship with her. But though Robert did not want to see Lucchesi immediately, he decided to tell Gemma the whole story. Meanwhile he must pack his bag without delay, for the coach left for Bologna in half an hour. He was spending one night in Bologna and then taking the train to Florence where he was meeting Gemma before lunch the next day.

Chapter 5

THERE WAS MICHELANGELO'S DAVID — OR MORE PRECISELY, THE facsimile of the David — against the brick wall of the Signoria; there was Cellini's even more wonderful Perseus under the corner of the Loggia dei Lanzi, but where was the mane of black hair that Robert was seeking? Gemma was not waiting at the trysting place — the open-air café nearest to the Lanzia. Robert was ten minutes late as his train had been late, and for two or three minutes he was a prey to an agony of anxiety. When the waiter came to rest beside his table he was in such agitation that he did not know whether to order a drink or not and waved him away. Suddenly he saw Gemma coming down the steps of the Lanzia; she had been looking at the figures round the base of the Perseus. She held out a cool hand to him across the table and he saw that on the third finger was a plain gold ring. They shook hands and sat down.

"I have taken a room for five days for myself and my husband," she said, and her dark eyes rested on him with an expression of gentleness and confidence which he never forgot. They drank the dry Martini vermouth with lemon peel that the waiter brought them and then Gemma led the way to a neighboring restaurant, the Grotta Guelpha, where they ate. But Robert was in a trance and could find no words. When they had eaten, Gemma took him over the Ponte Vecchio to the room she had taken at the top of an old house, the lower floors of which were occupied by joiners making reproduction furniture by hand, furniture that was the equal of the antique models which they copied.

For years afterwards the smell of wood shavings and of glue made Robert's heart beat faster, bringing back the old house in Florence and the room in which for the first time he had fully understood the intoxication of happy love.

It was being two and not one; yet one, part of the time: the two seeing, tasting, touching, smelling the same things simultaneously; laughing and chattering together; every external thing sparkling with new freshness because seen by two. That was love. Love to be pictured not by two figures in an interlocked embrace of mutual possession, but by two figures side by side: eager, darting forward like dolphins in the sea leaping, leaping and turning the flying fish of experience to one another.

The room Gemma had found was gaunt and bare, with walls of rough unpainted plaster, cracked in places, the floor of noble boards unswept and unpolished. It was sparsely furnished with a big double bed, a worm-eaten walnut table and three chairs painted green and touched here and there with gilding. There was a mirror on the wall, but no wash basin and no bathroom. In order to wash they had to cross the bridge and go to the baths, which rather to Robert's surprise, were scrupulously clean and supplied with abundant hot water. But this bare room was like heaven.

The big window opened out with a view over the roofs of Florence. Below them was the Piazza San Spirito and beyond a glimpse of the river and the dome of the cathedral. In this room Gemma and Robert lived and loved for three days, going out for coffee and rolls and then spending the morning separately: Gemma choosing the recordings she wanted for the concert, Robert in the picture galleries and churches. At one o'clock they lunched together, drank coffee at leisure, and made their way back slowly across the Ponte Vecchio to enjoy the siesta in their room.

Not until after sunset did they sally out once more to dine in a restaurant and then take their coffee and a glass of brandy or *grappa* in the open air.

During the three days and nights they spent in Florence, a sense of having thrown off a previous unworthiness and a knowledge that henceforward his love would be equal to Gemma's, lifted Robert into a state of exaltation which he had never known before. The belief that the only hope for success in love was in the subjugation and domination of a

woman, that otherwise man would be the slave of her ca-
price, was gone forever. The act of love had become a mys-
tical, or religious, shared experience of a force outside the
pair of lovers and beyond comprehension or analysis. He
would learn to give as much as he received: but whether he
did or not, he knew that his physical passion was noble because nothing was held back. And when Robert suddenly
remembered Caroline Stephenson, it was with surprise because she had retreated so far into the distance; because he
could see her for the first time with detachment. His view
of her had not been wrong but only incomplete. It was true
that she was somehow less earthbound than other women;
that she was irradiated with a strange light; that she had the
softness of a rose and the hardness of a polished flint; that
she was like a Greek immortal and a woman in Shakespeare.
All that was quite true. But compared with Gemma she was
grasping, and for that reason the nature of love eluded her.
The old nursery jingle came into his mind about children
born on different days of the week. "Monday's child is
full of woe, Tuesday's child has far to go," and then, "Friday's child is loving and giving" — and only those endowed
like Friday's children understand the mystery and happiness
of love and so justify their existence.

Gemma was more loving and giving than he could ever
hope to be himself, but she was not so completely transfig-
ured. Her passion was mixed with physical intuition; she

had a cool delight in the art of making love; realizing herself most fully by playing upon his body as though it were a violin, an instrument from which she could draw every possible note of vibrating ecstasy.

"Why should we ever go back to that little town with its sinister undercurrents of intrigue?" said Robert, turning to Gemma one evening as the sunlight on the walls of the houses on the opposite side of the street showed that the sun was nearly setting and that it was time for them to arouse themselves and go out to eat.

"Do you think that I can abandon my father? Such treachery would make me worse than Ercole or Angelo, or that nasty priest Mangoni."

"When we go back you must marry me. We must live openly together."

Gemma shook her head. "No. It is not impossible that we might marry one day. But not yet. I am not sure that there are enough things outside our physical passion to hold us together. I want you to know my character and your own better. And then there is another difficulty and for me a very real one. We are neither of us Catholics. Of course I was christened and took my first Communion as a little girl. But we should have to be married in church, simply because my father is mayor and keeps a shop. Everyone in the town knows that he is a freethinker. But he attends services because he is the mayor of the town. He compromises, and if we are to live in San Frediano, or the Romagna, we shall have to compromise too. And I don't like it." Gemma's face was serious and dark with pride.

"I don't like it either," said Robert. "I wasn't even christened. Surely we could have a civil marriage?"

"Absolutely impossible while my father is mayor and keeps a shop and is moreover an anti-Communist. We should be denounced from the pulpit by Father Mangoni and my father's shop would be boycotted and he would be ruined."

"It's like the middle ages."

"It is the middle ages — but with one difference. There is complete tolerance so long as one tells a few lies and goes through a few motions. Only, unfortunately, I dislike lies."

"The trouble is that if we can't live openly together I may do something on impulse that will upset the apple-cart," said Robert.

"I have taken the risk of that already."

Robert embraced her. "I know you have, my darling, and I can never love you enough for it. But the more I love you the more intolerable an intrigue or call it a secret relationship — becomes."

"I shall tell my father that you want to marry me and that will make our position much easier."

"I hope it will. I suppose it will secure our base. We shan't have to worry so much about Ercole's researches and Angelo's possible machinations."

"You leave out of account that I love my father more than anyone in the world and that he is not in very good health and that I am everything to him."

Robert clenched his fists and shook them in her face. "No, I don't. I am not trying to carry you away from your father. I don't feel jealous, possessive love. But how long shall we have to wait before we can always be with each other?"

"You wouldn't think three or four years unreasonable, I suppose?" said Gemma, assuming a sulky pout. "Or perhaps till my father retires in ten years time?"

Robert looked at her and saw a glint of laughter in her eyes. "I'll tear you into little pieces if you dare tease me, you Italian hellcat." Gemma stroked his hair and nestled closer.

Next morning Gemma left by the early bus which would take her to Forlì, where she changed for San Frediano, and Robert took the train to Bologna a little afterwards. When he arrived, he went and checked in at his hotel and left his bag there and then strolled out to have a drink under the arcades of the Palazzo del Podesta. He was sipping his second dry Martini vermouth with a lump of ice and a curl of lemon peel in it, when he suddenly saw Ercole Beccofilandria, who had apparently not recognized him. Robert decided instantly on his course of action.

"*Ciao!*" he called out — a greeting which is reserved only for intimates.

Ercole positively gaped at him with surprise, and his expression was borne out by his first words.

"So you have been here all the time! I never thought you had gone to Bologna at all, in spite of what I heard."

"As a matter of fact I haven't been here all the time — I've only just got back from a visit to Ravenna. But what are you doing here?"

Oddly enough Ercole was a much worse hand at improvising lies than Robert and the question obviously embarrassed him.

"Oh — my father wanted me to buy some veterinary instruments for him — it was a chance to visit Bologna."

Robert pointed to the chair opposite and Ercole sat down.

"My dear fellow, you are hiding something," said Robert. "I should suspect you were doing a bit of snooping in this city, except that the Bolognese are all so respectable."

Ercole tried to laugh; the amused cynicism of Robert's tone took him by surprise. He ended by blurting out the truth.

"San Frediano is a bit too hot for me just now. I've played some more of my jokes and I thought I would lie low until the dust settled."

"Photography or bird-watching? Or a bit of each?" asked Robert. Ercole nearly jumped out of his skin at the question, but managed a laugh which registered his profound uneasiness.

"You seem to know everything," he said at last with a touch of taking offense in his voice.

"No I don't. That is why I should like you to come and have a good dinner with me at Papagallo's and tell me the whole story. I am sure it's very amusing."

Ercole would have liked to escape from Robert, but the invitation was one which he could not bring himself to refuse. He would have told every secret he had ever heard and have sacrificed every shred of reputation he had ever possessed for a dinner at Papagallo's. But there are two restaurants of that name in Bologna, and Ercole asked cautiously, "You mean the real Papagallo's, don't you? Not the other one?"

"The real Papagallo's and the best meal that Bologna can provide. I'll book a table on the raised floor. Let's meet at eight-thirty."

The atmosphere of Papagallo's is that of professional distinction. The walls are lined with the autographed photographs of satisfied and replete patrons — yet a strict discipline confines the maître d'hôtel and his squad of waiters to a purely professional relationship. There is indeed so little of the Rabelaisian that one wonders at what moment in the course of the meal a Marconi, or a Karsavina, a Gigli or a Lollobrigida has had the nerve to unwrap the inscribed photograph from its string and brown paper and offer it to the stern master of the gastronomic ceremonies. For surely that severe figure would never take the initiative by asking for one?

These surroundings evoked all Ercole's snobbery and sense of inferiority. Yet his happiness was extreme and was increased by Robert's deferring to his judgment and describing him to the maître d'hôtel as a connoisseur of food and drink.

Both Robert and his victim ate and drank far too much. They started with *tortellini alla panna,* of a perfection to be found nowhere else, and quails with rice. After that *vol-au-vent* and *zabaglione.* The San Giovese wine was better than Robert expected and far better than Ercole had ever drunk before. In these circumstances it was not difficult to draw out the Thersites of San Frediano. He had said to himself before meeting Robert for dinner, "After all I need not tell him everything — I can always string him along."

But that was precisely what Ercole could not do. Of course all his activities were described as the practical jokes of an honest fellow who detested hypocrisy, but nevertheless the facts came out. Ercole had secured compromising photographs of a number of his fellow citizens and had sold them to Angelo. After which he had thought it best to make himself scarce. This indeed he had only been able to do thanks to the money Angelo had paid him.

"Some of my snaps were pretty hot stuff too. I got one of the doctor's younger daughter with the gardener's boy and a flashlight of the colonel of *carabinieri* with the bank manager's wife *en déshabillé*. Altogether it's not a bad collection."

"I suppose Signor Angelo appreciates them."

"They tickle him pink. Of course I feel a certain delicacy — some scruples. But then they are all such scum, what the hell does it matter to anyone?"

"I must say I feel sorry for the gardener's boy. He will certainly get the sack and he had a most agreeable job."

"His talents won't go unappreciated when the married ladies get to hear of them."

"A photographic Decameron," said Robert sententiously. "You must let me look through it one day, if the plague ever strikes San Frediano."

"Ha! Ha! Ha! A plague — I think it has broken out already. That is really why I'm here," said Ercole.

"Well, I don't want to catch it," said Robert. "I would rather stay here in Bologna listening to the modern Boccaccio. You've got the negatives here I suppose?"

"Yes, I only sold Angelo enlargements of each of them."

"I would like to give the whole series to Papagallo. They would make the decorations of his rooms much more amusing."

"You're so witty that I can refuse you nothing," said Ercole, as they left the restaurant. The maître d'hôtel managed a rather chilly bow. He had not listened to a word of the conversation, but Ercole's accent had grated on his ear and he neither expected nor wished ever to see him again.

After Papagallo's, they went to a café and drank brandy. Eventually Ercole was drunk and Robert had to help him into a cab and take him back to his lodging in a miserable little hotel. There Robert took off Ercole's shoes and trousers and put him to bed, wiped his forehead with a wet handkerchief, and looked about the room. In the bottom drawer of the wardrobe, he found an old imitation crocodile skin folder which looked promising. One look showed it contained strips of Leica film and some prints. Robert turned out the light, put it in his pocket and went back to his hotel with his prize.

After he had held a few of them up to the light he wrote the following note:

DEAR ERCOLE,

I enclose thirty-five thousand lire for the collection of photographs as agreed last night. As you have now sold them twice over, you will realize that they have not the same exclusive value. However, I won't mention my acquisition to Angelo, as I don't want to make trouble between you. I hope it won't be too long before the dust settles and you feel able to return to San Frediano.

Yours amicably,
ROBERT HARCOURT.

Then after bolting and locking his room, he went to bed and fell fast asleep immediately.

Next morning, as soon as Robert woke up, he seized Ercole's packet of photographs and opened it. The collection

75

was carefully indexed in alphabetical order and the negatives themselves, and a few print enlargements were contained in separate envelopes. Robert looked through the list of names. Gemma's was among them, but not her father's, or the schoolmaster's.

For some time a sense of shame prevented Robert from looking at the photographs; indeed, he felt for a moment a strong inclination to burn them. Then he reflected that if he did so he would destroy the evidence against Angelo who must have bought them in order to blackmail their subjects. But if he preserved them, to whom should he show them? Not to the bishop, though he would tell him of their existence. Possibly one day to Lucchesi. And where should he hide them until the time came for him to make use of them? There was no place in his lodgings in San Frediano which Angelo could not ransack if he were determined to do so.

Robert felt convinced that Ercole would accept the money that he had sent him and that he would hear no more from him for a week or two. But it was highly probable that he would tell Angelo that he had been robbed of his collection — and Angelo would stick at nothing to get it out of his hands. Robert took out the envelope marked *Gemma Lucchesi* and cut her name off the index. Then he switched on his bedside lamp, and taking the two little Leica negatives out of their envelope, he held them up to the light.

The first photograph, obviously a flashlight and taken at

night, was a close-up of Gemma, stark-naked, knee-deep in the waters of a lake or a pond. A dark blob in the distance, and out of focus, seemed to be the head of a man bathing with her. But it might equally, as far as Robert could make out from the negative, have been a stump of wood, or a dog, or a black stone. The other negative showed two girls, partly naked, asleep under an olive tree. Gemma — it was Gemma — had her head turned away and in shadow. Her breasts were bare, and the other woman, whom Robert had never seen and who did not look Italian, had her hand cupped round one of them. Robert looked at them for a long time. Then he put them in his billfold, packed up his belongings, paid his bill and left his hotel.

Before he left Bologna, Robert bought an envelope big enough to contain Ercole's collection. This he sealed up carefully with wax using his own signet, addressed it to himself and left it at the Bologna Office of the American Express Company with instructions that it was to be held until he called for it personally. He was afraid that Ercole, expecting him to take the Forlì bus, would be watching the coach station, so he hired a car to take him as far as San Lazzaro, and took the coach to Forlì from there.

Signora Salerno was unfeignedly glad to see him and had much to tell him. But nothing in what she said, or in what he could see out of the window, indicated that San Frediano was suffering from the plague or in the throes of revolution.

77

Chapter 6

Angelo is confident that the concert will be an enormous success and talked today about making it a monthly institution through the winter. He said to me today, 'I will win everyone with the musica.' It is rather comic, isn't it?" said Gemma.

Robert was sitting talking to her after dinner in the room over the shop; Lucchesi was reading in a far corner of the room. After the young people had been talking for a little, he stopped reading, put his hearing aid into his ear and listened intently to what they were saying.

"Aren't you pleased?" asked Gemma, though it was obvious that her lover wasn't.

"No. I'm not."

"What is it that you object to?"

"I detest Angelo and I don't like your seeing him."

"You aren't jealous by any chance?" said Gemma with an impish grin.

"Good God, no. I hadn't thought of him as a rival."

"I'm glad you are so confident. Because it would be ridiculous and I should feel ashamed of your intelligence if you were jealous. Though, as a matter of fact, Angelo is a very attractive man."

"I detest him and don't like your seeing him," repeated Robert.

"What reason?"

"He's a thug and a brute and dishonest and unclean."

"Why do you make accusations you know are exaggerated and which you can't prove?"

"I shall prove them. Though not tonight."

Robert had said nothing to Gemma about his meeting with Ercole in Bologna and he had no intention of doing so if he could avoid it. He had posted the negatives of Gemma to a friend of his in Paris, asking him to get enlargements printed — and had immediately felt ashamed of having done so. Gemma must have been aware of the flash when she was photographed after bathing. It was possible that she knew that Ercole had photographed her then. If he told her the whole story, she might ask if she was included in the collection — and it would be difficult to lie to her. And it would be impossible to tell the truth.

"You mean you can't prove your accusations and that you are talking nonsense."

"Do you remember objecting to my friendship with Ercole?"

"Of course I do. But he is a dirty creature; a degenerate . . . far worse than a rat — a parasite on rats, a louse, a tick sucking blood. Angelo is after all a man. He is clean. An animal out of the jungle, perhaps, but a fine one."

"You are unfair to Ercole. He is an intellectual, with a flair for the seamy side of life, which he sometimes deludes himself into thinking is a love of the truth. But I have given up my acquaintance with Ercole. Angelo is a hundred times more dangerous and I seriously dislike your seeing him."

"Really it is stupid to repeat yourself like this." Gemma shrugged her shoulders angrily.

Suddenly they became aware that Lucchesi was standing beside them.

"You must forgive me listening to your discussion — which is more important than the usual lovers' quarrel. Gemma, I agree entirely with what Robert has said. I am convinced that Angelo is not only an ambitious man but an unscrupulous and dangerous one. And though you are committed to producing this concert for him, I want you to take the greatest care in all your dealings with him."

"What do you actually mean by taking the greatest care? Do you want me to carry a pistol in my bag, or what?" asked Gemma in tones of extreme scorn, as though she were humoring an imbecile. Lucchesi laughed gently and his laugh was full of tenderness.

"No. Not a pistol. But you should be very careful not to

take any private letters in it of a kind you would not like Angelo, or his wife, to read and copy. You should not take your diary with you when you visit him, or your engagement book. That is what I mean by taking care."

Gemma said nothing, but her face flared in a blush so violent and so unsuited to her olive skin that both of the men found it painful to look at her.

"What do you say, Robert?" asked Lucchesi.

"I am very grateful to you for the warning and your support."

"I don't believe you are right," said Gemma. "But I will be guided by your advice. As a matter of fact . . ." She stopped as though regretting what she had said.

"As a matter of fact, what?" asked her father.

"Nothing . . . Only I did mislay my bag when I went there this morning. Signora Angelo found it for me."

Robert said nothing. It would, he thought, be a mistake to press the point that her father had made. Lucchesi apparently was of the same opinion, for he embraced his daughter tenderly, but without trying to reassure her, and then said good night in a tone in which, Robert thought, affection and irony were nicely balanced. Then he went to bed leaving the lovers to themselves.

The day before the concert, Robert observed a lady hurrying towards him across the piazza. He quickened his step to avoid her, but she began signaling with her umbrella, so that he was forced to wait for her. She was the doctor's wife.

"Oh, Signore, my husband and I are giving a little dinner party on Sunday to celebrate Gemma's triumph — for I'm sure the concert will be a success. We must make it one, mustn't we? We do so hope you'll join us. It will be in the upstairs room in the Belvedere Restaurant at nine o'clock." Robert accepted the invitation, reflecting that this was the lady who had cut him so markedly the morning after he had taken Gemma to the dance hall. Now it seemed she was going to the concert in the same hall. Robert speculated on the factors which had led to her change of attitude and the methods which Angelo might have employed to bring it about.

The following evening Robert was able to see that whatever they might be, they were effective. He had gone early and had taken a seat in the little gallery at the back of the salone, from which point he was able to see all the audience enter. It was the typical movie audience, composed of shop assistants, servants, shopkeepers and bourgeoisie. But it was remarkable because it included most of the notables of the little town, except the bishop.

Robert would have been ready to bet that all the subjects of Ercole's scabrous collection would be there. But when he saw them bustling in, one after another and taking their places in the best seats, drawing attention to themselves by signaling to their intimate friends and fellow victims, a feeling of nausea overcame him. Was this typical of the way the world was run? It was too foul. There was the bank manager's wife, with her husband beside her. Did he know that he was there because Angelo had a compromising photograph of his wife *en déshabillé?* Or had the wretched woman had to nag at him until he yielded? The doctor's wife and her two daughters were there — probably Robert would find himself placed between them the following night. But there was no sign of the gardener's boy. At the last moment a door opened and Father Mangoni slipped in to the gallery. He was obviously surprised to find anyone there. Robert bowed to him and got a stiff nod in reply. A moment later the door opened again and Signora Angelo came in. She went up at once to Robert and sat down beside him, giving him a rich smile.

"Dearest Gemma told me that I should be able to find you here and I've been wanting so much to have a *tête-à-tête.* We have so much to say to each other and I do want you to confide in me all about darling Gemma. She has no secrets from me and I know how much you mean to her."

But before Robert could reply, the opening bars of the music began.

Angelo, however, was not present, and his absence was confirmed during the interval when Gemma came on to the platform and announced that Signor Angelo had asked her to apologize for his absence as he was detained on business in Bologna, but that he had authorized her to say that he was ready to lend the hall once a month free of charge to the newly formed Musical Society, of which she was the honorary secretary. The price of the tickets of this and of future performances would go therefore entirely to the Society and be used to cover the expenses of hiring records — and she hoped it would not be long before there would be funds sufficient to engage world-famous performers. Her announcement was cheered and at the end of the concert there were a few cries for her to speak again, but as she did not appear they soon died away, as the audience began to troop out. Robert took pains to snub Signora Angelo as crushingly as he could, but it was impossible to criticize her husband for his part in the proceedings. He seemed to be both generous and disinterested. "Just as the bank manager seems to be here because of his love of music." Robert added to himself.

The morning after the concert, Robert paid Mr. Bannerman a visit at the hour when he might be expected to be found seated by his front gate staring out over the plain below.

The old man saw Robert approaching and watched him keenly.

"To what do I owe the pleasure?" he asked dryly.

"You asked me to drop in for a drink," shouted Robert

amiably, thinking that perhaps the old fellow was suffering from a lapse of memory and had forgotten him.

"So I did, but I've seen your friend Angelo since then, so I didn't expect to see you again. You can go back and tell him I've only one answer."

"I don't know what you are talking about," Robert shouted. "I went to Bologna on the day I last saw you and I haven't seen Angelo since I got back. Anyway I don't know that crook. I've only met him twice in my life."

"You are both Yanks, aren't you?"

"I am an American. Angelo is an Italian, isn't he?" yelled Robert and for the first time he wondered if perhaps Angelo was not an Italian after all.

"You say he didn't send you here?"

"I came hoping for a drink," shouted Robert.

"Didn't he send you the first time?"

"The first time I came here Signorina Lucchesi brought me and you didn't have the politeness to speak to either of us," Robert bellowed.

The old man grinned.

"I forgot that you are a friend of Lucchesi's. I apologize for suspecting you. The fact is I must be a bit jumpy. I'm getting too old for all this really," Mr. Bannerman confided cheerfully.

"What happened with Angelo?" shouted Robert. Then, as

Mr. Bannerman still seemed a trifle suspicious, he tried a last shout, "I believe that the fellow is a blackmailer and I'd like to know what you have to say."

"Blackmailer! He's a bloody Chicago gangster, if you ask me," said Mr. Bannerman excitedly. "The day after you came to see me, Mr. Angelo turned up and as quiet as you like asked me for the key of that gate." The old man turned and pointed with horror to the big iron gate standing ajar behind his chair. Then in a whisper, as though suddenly fearful of being overheard, he said, "Can you beat that for audacity? He calmly asked me for the key of that gate."

"What reason did he give?" asked Robert, forgetting to shout.

"Eh? I didn't catch that."

"What reason?" thundered Robert.

"I'm coming to that," answered Mr. Bannerman in his ordinary voice and then, rolling his eyes dramatically and gesticulating with his forefinger, he resumed his whisper.

"He asked for the key of my gate and said he felt responsible for preserving the peace. He said it might be necessary for him to put one of his men in my garden every night in case the Communists attacked me and that the charge for this protection would be forty thousand lire a month. If I didn't pay, he wouldn't like to guarantee my safety! And his wife is a Russian agent and the most powerful member of the Communist Party in the Romagna!"

"What did you say to him?" asked Robert after a pause.

"I told him that it was generally known in the town that I was a dead shot and that if I ever saw anyone inside my grounds without permission I would shoot to kill. I told him I was the last man to need protection in this part of Italy."

"What happened then?"

"He said that I was making a terrible mistake and that he was very sorry. He was terribly afraid that something was going to happen to me quite soon. So I pulled out my old naval forty-five Colt and said it would happen to the other fellow first. Then Mr. Angelo got into his big car and drove away."

"Well done," shouted Robert.

"Pooh. He's only a fourflusher," said Mr. Bannerman. "Come in and have a drink."

His wife had risen from the grass where she was sitting and helped her husband out of his chair. He locked his gate, took her arm and then, with Robert walking slowly beside them, they went back to the house in search of whisky.

At dinner that evening Robert had scarcely spoken to his neighbor on the right — the doctor's younger daughter — when he heard his *vis-à-vis* say in magisterial tones, "He seems to be that unfashionable thing in modern Italy: a strong man." It was the bank manager and his subject was obviously Angelo.

"If he isn't a Communist himself he wants to use the Communists. I have no doubt that he will get the Communist vote," said Lucchesi.

"Agreed. But he is the type who may very well save us from them," said the tax inspector.

"He is not so black as he is painted," said his wife.

"Really we all owe him a great debt of gratitude," said the doctor's wife.

"Yes, indeed. Without him dear Gemma could never have given us that delightful evening," said the doctor's elder daughter.

"What do you think?" asked Lucchesi, speaking to Robert across the table.

"I think he is the traditional Italian politician with whom we are familiar since Machiavelli," said Robert.

There was a general laugh in which a tone of gratitude was obvious. Robert had said what no one else wished to say.

"No! I protest. If there is one thing I will not allow to pass, it is cynicism," said the tax inspector.

"You see, you are rebuked publicly," said Gemma.

"I apologize. I was only seeking historical parallels — and I did not wish to choose them from a time that we can all remember," said Robert. There was a silence during which he wondered what Angelo had got on his card index relative to the tax inspector. All the vices were too venial or too attractive. It must therefore be something in the nature of a virtue, but a boring and a pompous one. It occurred to him that the inspector might be a Freemason. That would be a black mark against him under a Roman Catholic Minister of Finance. Could Ercole have secured a photograph of the tax inspector in his regalia, with trowel and apron?

"I can tell you one matter regarding which he showed generosity in an unexpected quarter," said the bank manager.

At the word "generosity" a feeling of constraint, not to say anxiety, fell upon the dinner party, for almost a third of the company had recently experienced unexpected generosity from Angelo. The bank manager drank a mouthful of wine and continued, "When Angelo took over the lease of the two lower floors of the palace and fitted them up as a dance hall, he had a completely new electric installation. While the men were doing the work he told Mangoni that he would pay for having the bishop's study and bedroom wired for power — he sent a workman upstairs to do the work and he had each room fitted with electric oil radiators and he paid for it all. Before that our good bishop used a *scaldino* in winter."

"That was certainly generous of him and the bishop was right to accept," said the doctor's wife.

"I don't think you can discover an ulterior motive there, Signore," said the schoolmaster. Robert did not reply.

"Did you enjoy your visit — was it to Bologna?" asked his

neighbor, the doctor's younger daughter, glancing at him with her black eyes and shading them with long black eyelashes. Yes, she was an attractive creature, just as a purple *aubergine* is an attractive vegetable.

"Indeed I did. But I went also to Ferrara, Ravenna and Padua . . ." Robert was about to embark upon a description of his tour and of the beauty of the Giottos in Padua, when he became aware of a sententious clearing of the throat and of the diners leaning over the table to catch every word of the verdict about to be pronounced. The bank manager was the spokesman of the company.

"I am sure we all agree that the real question is: Can we make Signor Angelo one of us? Of course he comes back to Italy — to our smaller world, with its older traditions — rather out of touch with some of our ways of thought, but I am optimistic enough to feel confident that, given a little time, the answer will be in the affirmative."

"The same question, of course, applies to Signora Angelo," said Robert.

There was a silence of consternation.

Angelo's wife had been conveniently forgotten.

"I move that this essentially technical question be referred to a subcommittee of the ladies here present," said Lucchesi. All the company laughed with relief.

Chapter 7

Next morning was market day and from his bedroom window Robert watched the street leading up to the piazza and listened to the cries of the market people until he saw Gemma coming up it carrying a large basket on her arm. Then he slipped downstairs and hurried to her father's shop. Luckily Lucchesi was alone, except for the boy he employed as an assistant.

"Come upstairs if you want to talk to me in private. Gemma won't be back for three quarters of an hour. She is going to buy fish, which means comparing every fish in the market — and then there are the vegetables and fruit." And Lucchesi took off his white coat and put on his jacket.

"You know that I want to marry Gemma," said Robert when they had sat down in the big living room. It was the first time that he had spoken to her father of marriage, and he found himself unexpectedly embarrassed because the little man listened, polite and perfectly impassive, as though he were being asked to prescribe professionally for some common ailment. If only Lucchesi would betray some emotion, if he would make some hearty and conventional response, how much easier it would be. Robert liked him and was confident that the little man returned the feeling. If he was ever going to say so, this surely was the time! But he said nothing whatever, and for once Robert had the sensation of being utterly baffled that comes at rare and unexpected moments to Americans in dealing with Europeans. And it was particularly strange because Robert was himself almost completely Europeanized and only half American. There was nothing for it but for him to flounder on, explaining that before the marriage he intended to visit America in order to see his half-sister and persuade her to agree to breaking a trust settlement. Lucchesi showed such polite indifference to these monetary affairs that very soon Robert was glad to change the subject.

"But I want to talk to you about all sorts of other things as well and perhaps this is a good opportunity. One of them — the least important I suppose — but I want to study it and write a book about it — is: has it ever occurred to you that there is a cult of Diana still persisting in this town? That the Madonna in the cathedral is really Diana and not the Virgin Mary, Mother of Jesus?"

At these words Lucchesi's eyes almost popped out of his head and his mouth actually dropped open for two seconds.

Robert waited, but it was some moments before the mayor of San Frediano seemed able to reply. At last he said in a low voice, "It is perfectly true. But it is a secret which nobody knows. All — or perhaps I should say — the vast majority of the votaries of Diana, are unaware of it. They believe in 'la Nostra Vergine' or 'la Madonna Nostra' and they would not pray to any other image. There are just a few of the better-off peasant-farmer class who have an inkling of the secrets of the old religion and that she is Diana and not Mary. But I think that the only two people who fully realize that 'our Virgin' is Diana are Father Anselmo and myself. Anselmo is a profoundly learned archeologist, with a great knowledge of folklore."

"The bishop knows because I talked to him about it. He is quite tolerant of it."

"He has been told a little — enough to prevent his being a nuisance, but not everything. But how did you find out?"

"It is as plain as the nose on your face."

At these words Lucchesi distracted Robert's attention by rubbing his nose thoughtfully and scratching it. Then he said, "Yes. But most people don't see the nose on their face. The obvious is what is overlooked. And this isn't really at all obvious to people living here."

"The Madonna is actually holding a female child by the hand — not a boy."

"What makes you say that?" Lucchesi asked fiercely.

93

"Well — it's partly a guess. But I am sure it is intended as a girl and is regarded as one by the worshipers."

"The child not only looks like a girl," said Lucchesi slowly. "But it is one. If you took off all her clothes, you would find the wax image was modeled sexually as a female. She is at least four hundred years old. Only Anselmo and I know that. Now you have guessed it."

"I can see that for an ardent Catholic like Mangoni such a detail might be important," said Robert and went on, "but it is really only a trifling indication. The real point surely is that it has become a woman's religion. No man prays to that Virgin."

"You are wrong there. The shepherds pray to her if there is snow and at lambing time. And I have known a sports-man take a hunting dog with hard-pad into the cathedral and pray for it, to the virgin huntress." There was a pause. Then Lucchesi said, "I hope you understand that if you want to live in Italy and to marry Gemma, you must never talk about your discovery, or publish anything about it. You would shock everyone and they would think that you were mad."

Robert stared blankly. He was already planning a book on it. Seeing that his word had come as a shock, Lucchesi continued, "Surely you can see that you would be torn to pieces, like Actaeon? Because although the cult exists, it is unconscious. And another reason is that Gemma would never marry you, and would never forgive you."

"But Gemma can't seriously worship Diana even unconsciously, I mean she isn't at all religious," exclaimed Robert. It suddenly seemed to him to be crazy that this fascinating survival should come into his personal life, and that the girl he intended to marry should worship a heathen goddess.

"Gemma isn't a Catholic. But she is far more than any of the other girls, or was until recently, a follower of the Dianic cult. Get her to tell you about it. But though it is unconscious among all except a few of the most primitive, it has a strong hold, and arouses something which is latent in the Italian woman's character. A curious thing is that the cult of our Virgin is stronger now than at any time since the Napoleonic wars. Perhaps it is a reaction against war and the armies of men invading Italy, and because the church was so powerless against war."

"How do you come to know about it?" asked Robert.

"Well. I know partly because the witches in the mountains use certain drugs in certain secret ceremonies which I procure for them. They used to gather the plants and distil them, but owing to deforestation they no longer grow in the district. Then I found out much more because I made use of one of these women when I was a partisan leader. But the girls praying in the Cathedral would be profoundly shocked if you pointed out that they had anything in common with the witches in the mountains. So, for your own sake and for Gemma's I entreat you to keep your mouth shut. Was there anything else you wanted to talk to me about?"

"Well, first of all, can one believe what old Bannerman tells one?"

"I should think so. He has no imagination."

"For example, he told me a story about your preventing his wife from poisoning him by giving her soda when she asked for cyanide."

"That is quite true. But it happened a very long time ago. I thought he had forgotten all about it."

"What a thing to forget," exclaimed Robert. "Then he told me that Angelo had been to see him just the other day and had asked him to pay forty thousand lire a month as protection. Can that possibly be true?"

"If Bannerman says so, it almost certainly is. But the old chap has only himself to blame. Everyone in the district for fifteen kilometers round believes that he keeps an enormous sum of money in his safe. And I daresay he does. Rumor puts it at three million lire or more. Some people say five million. If he banked all his cash and left his safe unlocked, there would be no question of 'protection.' As it is, one day, when he is dead drunk there will be a burglary. But is that all?"

"The other thing is that Bannerman says that Mrs. Angelo

is a Russian agent and that she is the most important Communist in the Romagna. Is that true?"

"I believe she is a Russian, or possibly a Lett. But she's not in the least important in the Italian Communist Party. I suspect that she was put here to report to Moscow as an independent check-up on the Italian Communists of the Romagna, and that she also watches Angelo and makes him toe the party line."

"Bannerman says that Angelo is an American. 'A Chicago gangster' are his actual words."

"That is extremely interesting. He is quite possibly right. In fact now that you say so I feel sure that he is. But it had not dawned on me."

"How would an old deaf foreigner like Bannerman, who can barely talk Italian, know all these things?" asked Robert.

"He has lived here a very long time and I think he has better sources of information than anyone; his wife's clan were the poorest and most criminal family in San Frediano. When Angelo came, he enrolled them in his gang and since then the police have rather given up arresting them, though I ask awkward questions if their immunity seems too flagrant. Bannerman gets everything they know. Of course he wouldn't know a thing about Diana, as he isn't interested in folklore or comparative religion. Indeed he's most bigoted."

" 'To hell with the Pope!' " quoted Robert. Lucchesi frowned and nodded. The words offended him.

"Now I must go," said Robert, adding, "I hope you don't object to me as a son-in-law." Lucchesi shook his head gently.

"If you make Gemma happy, you make me happy," he said.

After leaving his prospective father-in-law, Robert thought that he would walk up to the palace and talk to the old bishop, for he had certainly collected a lot of information about Angelo in a short time. But directly he stepped into the street he met Gemma bringing back her market purchases.

"Look at this fish!" she cried happily. "It's for supper and you must come and eat it with us. Now I'll put these things upstairs and you must come for a walk with me. It's so lovely." When she came back she caught hold of him and as they walked together across the piazza, hand in hand, she kept calling out to the stall holders and the old women bargaining, or passing the time of day, and they broke off to answer her and to admire her looks and to tell one another how happy she seemed with her handsome new *innamarato*. As the two lovers walked across the market square they were saluted by flashing smiles from everyone. There was not a sullen or an indifferent face in the whole chaffering crowd. Robert and Gemma brought with them a universal feeling of genuine delight, expressed in dozens of pairs of flashing dark eyes and grinning sets of flashing teeth. Like the autumn sun shining down from the pale cloudless sky and filling the streets with summer warmth, they gave to everyone the illusion that life was good and happiness the lot of man.

Gemma's spontaneous gaiety, following her father's revelation that she was one of the worshipers of Diana, kept Robert silent until they had left the town to walk along a field path towards a spur of the mountain where he had never gone before. He knew that he must speak, but he was very loath to break in upon her mood. But at last he felt that if they were to have the only relationship which mattered — that of complete intimacy holding back nothing from each other, he must speak to her of what he had discovered about the Dianic cult.

"I have never seen you among the women worshiping '*la nostra Vergine*' in the cathedral," he said suddenly.

"Did you expect to? I am happy and have no troubles to lay before her," said Gemma lightly, and added with curiosity, "but do you go often into the cathedral yourself?"

"I go there almost every day. Because it seems to me that the figure they worship is not Mary who lived in Bethlehem, but the 'Queen and huntress, chaste and fair,' of Ben Jonson's little poem which I read to you in Florence."

Gemma turned her head and looking at him almost coquettishly, said, "You sometimes frighten me with your intelligence."

"So you admit that '*nostra Vergine*' standing on the crescent moon, on the very spot where the image of Diana was worshiped two thousand — possibly even three thousand years ago — and holding a *female* child by the hand, is Diana?"

Gemma looked at him with a trace of something hidden or anxious in her expression. "So what?" she asked, using the English words.

"I know you are not a practicing Catholic yourself, but what emotion do you feel when you see those women and girls praying so passionately to a goddess who has survived in secret, after the demolition of her temple, sixteen hundred years of Christianity?"

"I feel . . ." Gemma hesitated, and then speaking rapidly she said, "I feel tremendously reassured. Sometimes I have a mad longing to awaken them to the reality of their worship. And when I have gone out into the moonlight with a certain woman in the mountains I have gone back into the strange world of two or three thousand years ago, a world in which there is no Heaven or Hell or tortured Christ, no cruel murders and senseless wars, no sense of guilt, no sin, or shame and in which I am at one with Nature."

"Could you feel like that if I were there, Gemma?"

"Not exactly. I feel a sense of fulfillment with you. But it is too hot . . . too personal. You possess me, and I possess you. You master me and I break you into pieces and make you my slave. But in the moonlight, where there is no man, everything is cool, everything is wild, everything is eternal. The wild beasts belong to Diana. It is dark, or it is moonlight and there is a girl's voice crying out by the waterfall or in the woods. An owl hoots in answer. Then, for the first time one is completely aware of oneself and one is not afraid of what one has found. A woman who has not experienced it has never completely lived."

Gemma was silent and they walked for some way without speaking.

"Do you understand what I have tried to say? Do you understand without being jealous? You need not be. Because if I had not experienced these emotions I could not love you one tenth as much as I do. Love would be — as it is to many women — all bedclothes and bolsters and mattresses. Whereas for me love is shot with the memory of reflections in a lake at midnight, of feeling the goddess's tresses brush my shoulder in the darkness, of rolling naked in the dew-soaked grass when I am hot with running, of feeling the moist muzzle of a hound touching my cheek and waking me when I am lying alone among the forest ferns."

Robert squeezed her hand. "I understand." And he felt that in truth he did understand even though he was saying to himself: "But there is no forest and there are no ferns."

Gemma was looking at him with gratitude but somehow completely exhausted by trying to put her emotion into words.

"Please, Robert, don't let's talk about it again — or not for a very long time. But remember, if you sometimes feel angry with me, that you chose to have a madwoman rather than a mattress."

Robert had been so preoccupied with what Gemma had been saying that he had not noticed where she was leading him. Now he found that they were standing on a level space that jutted out on a spur of the mountainside. It was dotted with juniper bushes and there were many huge rocks. It was one of those natural yet almost artificially theatrical places which so many early Italian painters chose as the setting for their scenes.

Gemma led him between two huge overlapping rocks to where there was a space of green sward, and almost miraculously, water bubbled from the mountainside and fell in a thin waterfall into a little rock pool. In the shade of the rock there were green plants in striking contrast to the cistus and withered rock-roses of the sun-baked slopes beyond.

"This is Diana's pool. I have never seen a man here before. And to prove that you love me and understand what I have told you, come and take me here."

Robert held Gemma by the shoulders and searched her face.

"You are not getting a kick out of some sort of sacrilege, offending your virgin goddess?"

For a moment Gemma looked at him almost contemptuously. "Don't be so stupid. You are my lover and I have brought you here because I believe that you can understand — really understand and accept — my religion, if it is a religion. Diana doesn't want a world full of old maids. If I have run wild in her moonlight, she will come to my help when I have a child. It is as simple as that."

Robert and Gemma undressed and out of the wind, on a flat sun-warmed rock, it was not too cold for them to lie naked and caress each other's bodies and to make love in a suddenly closed-in shuttered world, and then, panting, recover their senses and lie and talk, shifting their positions to ease the bruises their hard couch had inflicted on them. How black Gemma's hair was, spread out above her head upon the rock! How brown her swelling breasts! How slender the waist and flat the stomach which ran down between the hips to a patch of crisp black curls, a patch so small that it made her woman's body look almost immature. Then the solid peasant calves and the small feet. Every detail of her construction enchanted Robert.

"I'm not jealous of what we have been talking about, of what you have told me — but I am envious," he said.

"If the goddess had been watching us, she would have been envious of me," said Gemma.

At that moment a large white greyhound of a kind seldom seen today in Italy, but not uncommon in the pictures of the fourteenth and fifteenth centuries, trotted between the rocks past them and lapped water from the pool. Its thirst satisfied, the animal turned towards them and came up and laid its long narrow muzzle on Gemma's knee, sniffed inquisitively at her body and looked first at her and then at Robert with transparent amber eyes.

There was something so strange and so symbolic in the sudden appearance of the hound at that moment, that they could not speak of what they thought but stood up and put on their clothes in silence. Robert looked at his watch. It was late. Gemma wanted to hurry back. Her father would have had to find his own lunch but she would be in time to make him some coffee before he took a siesta.

As they went away, Robert noticed how the great rocks closed in around the sanctuary, so that no one crossing the spur would have suspected its existence — and when they had stepped down from the little plateau with its junipers and scattered rocks, there was only the perpetual panorama of rocky slopes rising from acacia thorn scrub and the vine-yards stretching down the lower slopes into the plain.

But before they parted Robert asked, "Was it on that dreadful night after the murder of your mother, when you escaped into the darkness, that you first felt this love for the night, and that you first became whatever it is that you are?"

Gemma shook her head quickly with a shudder of revulsion.

"No, no. Not then. But the day after my mother's murder,

my father took me into the high mountains where the Fascist bands and the Germans never came and gave me to the wife of a stonecutter to bring up. I lived with Giovanna until several months after the war, when Father could make some sort of a home again. She was an initiate — you can say that she was a witch — and it was she who initiated me into all the mysteries. You know I believe she sent that greyhound to show her approval." Gemma gave Robert an indescribably roguish, enigmatic look.

"You aren't horrified at my being brought up by a witch, are you? When we get married we will go up into the mountain and stay with her for our honeymoon. Now I must run if Father is to have any coffee while he reads the paper before his siesta."

Robert blew her a kiss and turned into the Belvedere to have lunch alone.

That afternoon Robert walked up to see the bishop. The old man looked tired and ill and though he received Robert graciously, he exploded at the first mention of Mr. Bannerman.

"I am surprised that you should visit such a vicious man. He is a scandal to our community. I never remember the text, 'the wicked flourish,' without thinking of that disgusting reprobate. He, who by upbringing and tradition, glories in the persecution of our good Irish Catholics, escaped internment and infallible ruin during the war owing to the accident of his having been born in what is now the Irish Republic. If there is one man in San Frediano whom I abhor it is that vicious, self-indulgent, bullying, drunken Protestant who seems to have enjoyed the especial protection of the devil for the last forty years."

Robert listened to this diatribe in silence and did not attempt to defend Mr. Bannerman. It would be a useless waste of breath and only exasperate the bishop further. As soon as he could he drew his attention to Angelo, telling him that Lucchesi was also convinced that Angelo was an American.

"Of course, of course. But it does not help matters if he is," said the bishop testily.

Robert, however, interrupted him to say that on the contrary if they could prove that Lucchesi were right, it would make all the difference to Angelo's future. And he explained that even if he had no criminal record, an American citizen could not enter into the active political life of another country. In particular he could not run for mayor, or hold any public office.

The bishop thumped the table at this.

"I am a stupid old fool. I see that it is enormously important and all the more because his wife is also a foreigner. I thank God for His having prompted me to enlist your help for, under providence, you may be in a position to save us. You alone seem qualified to find out the truth. You must go to America at once."

106

"I don't think I can," said Robert.

"I suppose you want to marry Lucchesi's daughter, don't you? But you would have to put it off anyhow. You can't do it till I agree," and the old man grinned maliciously. There'll have to be a dispensation. She's a Catholic — a bad one, I allow — and you're a heretic. But I'll have the dispensation waiting for you when you get back from America and I'll marry you in the cathedral myself. That's a bargain."

"We have made no decision; we have fixed no date," mumbled Robert unhappily. The bishop's offer was disconcerting. It would have to be refused — and yet unless it were accepted it seemed probable that Gemma and he could never be married at all. Robert had planned to go to America before he and Gemma got married. But first they must decide whether marriage was possible.

The interview with the bishop was going badly enough without his trying to explain their dilemma — their silly scruples about telling lies. Robert changed the subject by mentioning the existence of Ercole's snapshots, but without saying that he had secured them. The bishop once more exploded with wrath, "Ah! What horrors you unearth! What a pack of scoundrels inhabit this Italy of ours! Miserable sinners! I only hope that that villain Angelo will make them suffer as they deserve. Then, and then only, will there be some hope that the wretches will repent!"

The bishop was certainly in a bad mood and Robert regretted that he had gone to see him, a regret which increased when, on his taking leave, the old prelate, who was still flushed with indignation, said to him, "You must come back and see me in two days time and I shall expect you to tell me that you are going back to America at once to discover the truth about Angelo. It is your clear duty to do so."

He lifted his hand and Robert kissed the episcopal ring, although he had half a mind not to do so.

That night Robert lay awake thinking over the strange day that he had spent and came to two conclusions: that Gemma's intense romanticism, for her emotional attitude to the Dianic cult seemed to him nothing else, increased rather than diminished his love for her. He might easily have been irritated if he had felt it were false, or contemptuous if it were due to willful irrationality. But instead of either he felt tenderness for what was in essence a poetical enhancement of life.

But the bishop's firm intolerance had had precisely the opposite effect. He felt more than ever that it would be a waste of time to try and achieve an intimate friendship with the old man. From a rationalist standpoint there was nothing to choose between a belief in natural magic or a belief in holy relics and the miracles of the Roman Catholic Church. Yet for some obscure reason he was pleased rather than offended by Gemma's suggestion that the greyhound was a familiar sent by Giovanna to signify approval of their love-making, whereas the bishop's condemnation of Mr. Bannerman and his legalistic belief in ritual and Mr. Bannerman's fierce hostility to Catholicism aroused his dislike for them both. What was the reason? Was it that owing to its Semitic origin, Christianity was so often a persecuting religion, whereas coming from ancient Greece, the Dianic cult was not? Or was it because Christians condemned the sexual relationship as sinful, whereas he shared the attitude of Blake and of D. H. Lawrence, a veneration which was as strong in the ancient religion, as it still is in Hinduism? Before he fell asleep Robert's thoughts turned from the abstract to the concrete as he lived over again their love-making on the rock and felt again the kisses Gemma had given him that evening when they had parted after supper.

Chapter 8

A big V-8 pulled up with a squeal at the corner of the mountain road where Robert was sitting on a bank, looking out over the sunlit plain and waiting for Gemma, who had gone behind some bushes a few moments before. Angelo jumped out of the car, slammed the door, and giving Robert a warm smile, sat down on the bank half-facing him.

"It's a lucky chance. I wanted to see you."

"Oh, yes?" said Robert, but Angelo did not seem to notice his unfriendliness.

"I just back from Bologna. I see our young friend Ercole there," said Angelo in a sunny manner.

"Did he tell you that I had seen him there?" asked Robert.

"He's a bit sore with you, Mister. You go drinking with him and then, for a joke, you took his photos. He asked you now to give them back to me."

Robert smiled and shook his head. "Nothing doing." Angelo was plainly genuinely grieved by the refusal.

"Ah, Mister. You play fair and no one will quarrel with you. You play a joke and we laugh. But if you take advantage of a poor boy . . . you get him drunk and then steal his photos . . . that is not going to do you any good, Mister. You give them back."

Robert laughed and shook his head.

There was a pause while Angelo looked at him and then looked away at the sunlit landscape.

"Perhaps you think you can do what you like because Ercole's in Bologna and don't want to come back. But you make a big mistake. Ercole has a heap of friends — they will see he gets fair play. He's a nice kid — he would not like it if anything happened to you because of him. He wants to be friends with everybody."

Robert gave a guffaw.

"He sets about it in an odd way, if he wants to make himself popular. He told me he had made San Frediano too hot to hold him."

"The poor boy is his own enemy," said Angelo. There was a pause and then he asked gently and almost affectionately, "What you want to take his photos for?"

"Did Ercole tell you that I paid him thirty-five thousand lire for them?"

"That was too much, Mister. But I will give you your money back to stop any trouble. I will pay you out of my own pocket. I don't quarrel with any man about money. You give me those photos and we stay very good friends. If not, you make a heap of trouble for yourself."

"You are wasting your time," said Robert, in a more friendly tone than he had used up till then.

It was Angelo this time who shook his head — but to express a sort of puzzled regret.

"Tell me, what for you look for trouble?"

"I don't like blackmail, Mr. Angelo."

"Why you talk like that?"

Robert was silent and there was a long pause. At last Angelo said almost shyly, "Erocle tell me that there was two of Gemma. He say you keep those if that's what worries you, and I'll pay you back your money in full."

"You are a dirty hound, Angelo, but you won't do your dirty work here. You will leave this place and these people in peace," said Robert in a very quiet voice and trying to keep his self-control.

Angelo pursed his lips and shook his head with real regret.

"You make it very difficult. I am in business and in politics in this town. And they have to come first. You're an American. You must know business and politics come first. But I do wish it hadn't happened. Look here, Mister, I'll give you three days to think about it."

"Just as you like."

Angelo got up and walked to his car and seated himself in it. Then he opened the door, got out and walked back to where Robert was sitting and said with the utmost earnestness, "Don't think it isn't easy for me to make trouble for you, Mister. You know that old song 'I can do anything better than you can,' don't you? Well that goes for trouble. I've only to say the word and you're out. But I hate that sort of thing. Look how beautiful it all is . . ." and Angelo jerked his chin at the landscape below them.

"*A native Italian would have flung out his arm.*" Robert reflected as he watched, astonished by this appeal.

"Look . . . how peaceful . . . the sun shining . . . the light everywhere . . . lovely Italy. Why should we quarrel? You keep out of business and politics — you're not an Italian, Mister."

It was on the tip of Robert's tongue to say, "Are you one?" But he caught himself in time.

"You love that girl, Gemma. She is so sweet. There should be someone to look after her. I am asking you to think better of it, to keep out of politics and give Ercole back his photos."

Robert said nothing and Angelo walked back to his car irresolutely, got in, started the engine and drove away.

It had hardly disappeared when Gemma ran out of the bushes and asked excitedly, "What was that all about? You must tell me every word."

"Oh, it's nothing interesting. It's a bore really," said Robert, trying to gain the second or two in which to concoct something plausible.

"Tell me at once, every word he said," said Gemma, already furious.

"But it was nothing — a long rigmarole — how he was in Bologna and hadn't wanted to miss the concert, but business always had to come first . . . As an American I must know that business and politics always had to come first."

"It's no good, Robert. I don't believe you. You are lying," said Gemma. "But I will wring the truth out of you. It hurts me very much if you lie to me."

"I swear that those were his exact words. Then he said, 'Look how beautiful it all is . . . the sun shining . . . the light everywhere . . . lovely Italy . . . Everything is so peaceful.'"

"Can't you invent a better lie than that, you dolt?" cried Gemma, with her fury tempered by amazement. "Why, you must think that I'm a baby! I shall go straight to Angelo and ask him to tell me the truth since you won't. I mean it!" she added glaring at him.

Then, as Robert said nothing, she pounced upon him catching hold of him by both ears.

"I believe that you think that you are being chivalrous. You are hiding something unpleasant, or dangerous. I think that you are in trouble with him over something. It ought to be something to do with me — but I can't think there is, or can be anything."

Robert said nothing and Gemma, still holding him by the ears, shook his head to and fro with exasperation.

"Was it something about our going to Florence together? It could not matter, because I've told my father all about it."

Robert still said nothing. If Gemma was not going to believe his lies, it was better not to tell them.

"Well it seems you are dumb. If you won't tell me about it, will you tell my father? Otherwise I shall go to Angelo this minute and demand to know the truth."

"Yes, I'll tell your father all about it," said Robert.

Gemma let him go and sketched a gesture of the utmost despair.

"Darling, what hope is there for us if you are ready to tell my father but don't trust me, or respect me sufficiently to talk to me about something important? And why did you try to fob me off with such idiotic lies! Angelo raving about the beauties of nature — my foot."

"As a matter of fact his exact words were: 'Look how beautiful it is . . . the sun shining . . . the light on everything . . . lovely Italy!' I was a good deal surprised myself," said Robert, rubbing his ears.

"Well, you see what a nice man he is!" exclaimed Gemma, glaring at Robert again, for she was furious at being told she was wrong in this small point. It was, she felt, positively insulting of Robert to persist in trying to justify himself.

"Why do you want to quarrel with him? You are not even an Italian. Why do you go and get yourself mixed up with him and that dreadful creature Ercole over things that don't concern you?"

Their walk was ruined: the prospects of making love were nonexistent. Three quarters of an hour later an angry Gemma led Robert into the living room above the shop where her father was having luncheon by himself.

Tossing her head angrily she said, "Mr. Mayor, this young foreigner has promised to tell you the details of a mysterious conversation which I watched him having with Angelo and which he refuses to tell me about. I must warn you that he is a skillful liar. Don't be put off with nonsense. I have an idea that he has got himself mixed up in some unpleasantness. Be sure that you get the truth out of him." And Gemma marched with tremendous dignity out of the room, her back very straight and her eyes looking straight before her.

"What ridiculous airs she gives herself. She's a spoiled child," said her father. "Now we shall have to pacify her by concocting something, because I don't for a moment suppose that you wish to confide in me what you refuse to tell her."

Robert did not hesitate to tell Lucchesi the whole story of his discovery of Ercole engaged in snooping in the campanile, his acquisition of the photographs in Bologna and of Angelo's demand for them, and his indefinite threats of trouble.

116

While Robert talked Lucchesi sat perfectly still on a high stool. In his white coat, and blinking frequently through his thick lenses, he looked, Robert thought, like a white owl. And certainly no owl could have appeared wiser or more judicious than the mayor of San Frediano at that moment. After Robert had described how Angelo had given him three days to change his mind and had actually come back and pleaded with him not to run into trouble, Lucchesi commented, "It shows how safe he feels that you can make no use of the photographs at present. And of course he is right. You have no evidence whatever against him — except that he has suddenly become unexpectedly popular among a set of timid people. But I think you should leave here as soon as the three days are up. You mustn't run an unnecessary risk."

"You are in just as much danger as I am — if either of us is in any," said Robert.

"Be under no misapprehensions about that. Angelo is a serious character. When he says trouble he means what he says. But about myself — I am in more danger than you in the long run, but not, I think, at present. I shall have to be got rid of before the next elections — but not in a spectacular manner. Angelo wants to be put up as mayor and would probably not be elected if I were a candidate."

"But what can be done?" exclaimed Robert, aghast at Lucchesi's calm acceptance of his fate.

"A lot can be done and perhaps you are the man to do it."

And Lucchesi asked Robert if he would help him to investigate Angelo's past, of which he was suspicious.

"All I know is that he first appeared about two months after the Salerno landing, as a partisan in a group working about seventy kilometers from here. What makes me suspicious is that in those days English-speaking Italian partisans were rare birds. When this district was in liaison with the British Army, Angelo was most useful. But when American troops took their place, he vanished. I heard, later, that he had joined a Communist group further north. What strikes me as worth investigating is why a man who had lived in America and speaks American, always avoided contact with the American Army."

"You think he may be wanted for some crime in the States?"

"Something like that. When he came to live here a year ago, he told the *questura* that he was a native of Rimini, and his papers are those of a certain Gaetano Angelo born in Rimini in 1920. But if he is an Italian he comes from Calabria or Sicily — anyhow from south of Naples."

Robert then described his unsatisfactory visit to the bishop, who had told him that it was his duty to visit America immediately in order to discover the facts about Angelo. The foolish old man was actually expecting him to go, though it could not be of any use, since he had not enough facts about Angelo for him to be identified.

Lucchesi at once told Robert that he had everything that would be necessary to investigate Angelo's record: an excellent series of fingerprints. He had come into the shop one morning and had asked for a pick-me-up because he had a bad hangover. Lucchesi had given it him in a glass smeared with vaseline. He had also two excellent photographs of Angelo, his exact height and weight, his size in hats and shoes and his tailor's measurements.

"You are really asking me to go to America also, to see if I can trace him?" said Robert suddenly, and Lucchesi hesitatingly admitted that he agreed with the bishop.

"I don't like to use the word duty or to tell any man what it is his duty to do. But then I am not an ecclesiastic. All the same, for what I admit are partly selfish reasons, I wish you could go at once, and not as you would prefer, in two or three months' time."

After this Robert felt that there was nothing he could do but agree, and it was settled that he should leave San Frediano in three days' time and go to Washington to investigate Angelo's past before he went on to see his sister in New England. He had not been back to America for twelve years.

"Colonel Stephenson is in New York," said Lucchesi. "If you are in difficulties tell him the story; he will know what to do and how to help."

Robert smiled and tried to conceal his smile. It was ridiculous that an American should need the help of a British soldier in dealing with his own government. Nevertheless he wrote down Patrick Stephenson's address and promised to see him.

"Well, now I must tell Gemma all about it," said Robert, but her father objected. He thought it would be far better if she were not told the real reasons for Robert's journey.

"In the first place I don't want her to know that I believe that I am in danger myself. If she guessed that she would be extremely anxious — she might even refuse to go on seeing Angelo. Even if she continued her work with the Musical Society, her changed behavior would put Angelo on his guard. By letting her continue that work I think I am post-poning my immediate danger. A series of concerts are to be given before I am eliminated."

Lucchesi chuckled. "You know I find it most agreeable to imagine that my life is being prolonged by the works of Beethoven and Mozart? Then, so long as Gemma is seeing Angelo, I am to a certain extent being kept in touch with what he is doing and thinking. It is always most important to keep in touch with one's enemy. Quite apart from that, many other people are sure to ask her why you have gone back, and Gemma is a bad liar, so that people will scent a mystery."

"But if I don't tell her the truth what shall I say?" asked Robert in despair.

"Tell her what you told me the other day when you talked

about marriage — all about seeing your half-sister and breaking the trust."

"But what have we been talking about all this time?" asked Robert wildly.

"I don't think there would be any harm in your telling her about Ercole's photographs and about Angelo wanting to get hold of them. And by the way, it might be a good thing for you to borrow this. I have sometimes found a pistol very useful." And opening a drawer, Lucchesi took out a .32 Steyr automatic pistol and handed it to Robert.

"You can give it back to me when you leave here."

Robert told Gemma the story of Ercole's photographs and within a few hours was bitterly regretting it and telling himself that her father had proved himself an owl for having listened to him. Gemma was not only disgusted by the story, but angry with Robert for having mixed himself up with the matter.

It was also obvious from the first moment that Gemma did not believe that Robert was telling her the whole truth, and that she was wounded and offended. For if he were not telling the truth, it could only be because he did not completely love her, or entirely trust her. His feelings were therefore different in kind from hers. Looking back on their relationship, it seemed to her that they always had been. Her pride revolted — as it had before when something of the same sort had happened to her. If the whole truth were nothing but the loathsome story of Ercole's snooping and photography, it was incredible that Robert should have refused to tell her until after he had told her father. And then a possible and miserable reason for his reticence occurred to her. Perhaps her photograph had been among the others.

"Of course it was!" And Gemma remembered the sudden flare that had lit up the beach at Cesenatico at midnight when she had been bathing naked with Bettina. She had known that Ercole was in the little port that night and suspected he might be spying on them. It had not occurred to her that the sudden flare had been to take a flashlight photograph. Robert had said nothing. She could not. If he asked her, she would be too proud to explain. And she reflected that it was perhaps a pity that she had never said a word to him about her past love affair. If she had done so it would perhaps have led her to see Robert in his true light rather earlier. But he had never bothered to ask her, though it was obvious that she was not — for example — a virgin. Now it was too late ever to say anything. He would think she was trying to justify herself. Certainly it seemed to her that there was some subtle change in their relationship. Robert seemed to be very urgent and upset — and then he went off and avoided being with her all day.

For the three days left him — and he had not told Gemma of his immediate departure — Robert was extremely busy. First of all there was the business of raising enough money to pay for the ticket on the boat. He cabled from Forlì, as he did not want to start gossip in San Frediano — telling his bank to sell stock but in the meantime to book him a tourist ticket on the next Italian liner. Then from Forlì he took the bus to Bologna in order to retrieve Ercole's collection from the American Express office. Then he returned by the next coach.

When he got back to his room, it was obvious that it had been searched in his absence. It was already midnight, but he went round to Lucchesi's and there was a light in the room upstairs.

"Gemma's gone to bed with a headache," said the little man.

"I'll come in all the same," said Robert and Lucchesi whistled when he told him that he had Ercole's collection in his pocket.

"Better leave them with me for tonight. I'll put them with the poisons and narcotics in my safe and tomorrow I'll send them to a friend of mine in Rome who is in the Ministry of the Interior."

Robert handed over the sealed packet and went back to his room.

Signora Salerno, to judge by her snores, was sound asleep, but in the twenty minutes during which Robert had been absent, someone had searched his room again.

"I hope the fellow won't wake me up, but I'm so tired I

feel I could sleep through anything," Robert said to himself as he turned out the light. He did not wake until half past eight, but there had been no intruders during the night. After breakfast Robert went round to see Gemma, but she had left the house at dawn telling her father that she would not return until the evening.

Robert was leaving the next morning at eleven o'clock. With despair in his heart he walked up the hill to the bishop's palace. The little town was spread out below him bathed in the late November sunshine. Lovely Italy!

The old bishop was delighted to receive him; Father Mangoni was away "sitting for an examination." What examination? Robert asked himself. He accepted the old man's invitation to share his meal — it turned out to be dried cod with a white sauce and some delicious white grapes. But then, after the little courtesies had been exchanged, and he had said that he was leaving the following day, he found that he had nothing to say. After his last visit he had realized that the gulf between him and the bishop was too great for him to bridge. But the gulf was not unbridgeable from the other side and the old man did not hesitate to broach the subject.

"Your Musical Society has done a great deal to make Angelo popular, or tolerated, by respectable people. I know that he is a bad man, that he would commit any crime to get power, but I am terrified because I see he can make himself more liked by the people in this little world, than I, or any of the priests."

Robert shook his head. "I'll never believe a gangster can give people what they really want. He rules by terror and not by law."

"All rule by fear. Many of us, perhaps too many, care more for the church than for the populace, including the poor lost souls outside the church. I speak not only of their eternal salvation but of their lives here. Angelo can offer them more land, more money, more machines to do their work for them, more noise, more pleasure. He can make them believe in a world of ice-cream for the children, cosmetics for the girls, motor cars and aeroplanes for the young men, television for everyone. Only the deaf and the blind seem to be left out."

Robert said nothing, but after a time the bishop began to speak again, in a clearer, more certain voice, as though an illumination were coming to him as he spoke.

"I am always watching faces. I have done so all my life and have learned to know a good man or woman from a bad one. And on the summer evenings since the dancing started, I have watched the faces of the men and girls coming up in their hundreds every Saturday and Sunday evening. I have compared them with the faces of those coming to the cathedral for mass. The young people are no worse than those who come to pray in the cathedral. They sin — but they do not know it. They are simple and without hypocrisy. They come because they love noise and the bright lights and want to laugh and make love and be admired. But of those in the cathedral how many come because they have to be known to come to mass? Or because they want to be better than their neighbors, or out of long habit? A few, frightened by the death of a loved one, come sincerely seeking God. But otherwise most of them come for the same reason that the young people go to the dance hall — to see their friends, show off their best clothes and to be admired."

Robert said nothing and there was such a long silence that he wondered if the bishop were asleep. Then the old man added, "Would it matter to anybody — except God — if Angelo took my place? What difference is there between us except that he makes them happy with promises for this world that will not be fulfilled, and that I make them uneasy with promises of the next world which will?"

"The difference is that he seeks power by fear and you seek power by love," said Robert.

"Thank you for saying that, my son," said the bishop. He held out his hand with the palm uppermost, to be kissed.

Robert disliked the idea of meeting Angelo. He believed the man was a gangster — or at any rate a blackmailer. He was going to America at great inconvenience and expense earlier than he would otherwise have done to try and rake up the man's past and ruin him — and for that reason anything in the way of friendly human intercourse with him was repulsive. But there was no doubt that Angelo had tried to be friendly when they had last met. Robert hoped that he would be able to avoid him. But when he walked down the marble staircase into the interior courtyard, there was Angelo waiting for him by the lion fountain. He was smiling and sunny, and held out his hand so that it was very difficult for Robert to ignore it. But he did.

"I think you have got me wrong, Mister Harcourt. You talk yesterday about blackmail. See here. Ercole take the pictures — you know some people are queer one way, some the other. Well, Ercole a bit queer about pictures. He showed me them and I bought them. Then I go to see the people he had snapped and I give each of them back. I say, 'Here is a picture that bum Ercole took of you. I don't like such things myself, so here it is for you to tear up — and here are free seats for all your family to come to the concert. If you will bring them I shall feel more than repaid for my trouble with Ercole's nasty pictures. Yes, I shall think it very friendly of you.'" Angelo paused. "That's how it was," he said with a sigh. "And now you give me those photos."

"You want some more prints, I suppose," said Robert.

"I don't want to quarrel with you, Mister. But if the police found you with those photos, they would think you were in some racket with Ercole. They would expel you from Italy for a thing like that."

"How much would you charge me for protection, Angelo, if I were to run into trouble? I mean in danger from Communists, or anything like that?" asked Robert. Angelo stood motionless; the only thing that moved were his eyes, which flickered to and fro with the menacing speed of a snake's tongue. Robert had been hoping that he would make his enemy lose his temper, but he was disappointed. Angelo sighed deeply and his sigh said plainer than words could have done that he was only too well used to talking with fools and did his best to suffer them gladly.

"I don't think you are a Catholic, Mister Harcourt?" he asked.

"No, certainly not," said Robert.

"Then why you been up to see the old man?"

"I like him. He's kind to me, and he's a very honest man. We have tastes in common, also, which you haven't got."

"What do you mean?" asked Angelo. He wanted to get it quite clear.

"We like the same things: the old civilized traditional ways of living: certain standards of honor and decency. We hate life to be made ugly and evil."

"I guess you can treat yourself to all that if you've the dough," said Angelo uneasily.

"Not a bit of it. The peasants — the *contadini* — live in the way I mean. They work all the hours that it is light: work with their slow oxen, and if they can have wine and bread, pasta and salt cod and a watermelon and a bunch of grapes, they are happy. Life gives them the love of a woman, children, the knowledge of work well done."

"Your Pop ought to have raised you to be a bishop, son," said Angelo and spat reflectively. "You make a sermon on the text: 'Massey-Harris could bring you a Fergie, but you must plough with bullocks all your life.' Go and preach that to the peasants of an evening."

Robert laughed, but Angelo went on quickly.

"You read about opening up the West: well Italy's a country that needs opening up. You could step up production fifty per cent if you mechanized agriculture, and do it with a quarter of the labor."

"Yes. Of course that's coming. And American aid will bring it quickly."

Angelo shook his head. "The Russkis will beat the Yanks and the Commies will beat the Catholics."

"Possibly. But I was talking about values. Free men are better than slaves. Honest men are better than blackmailers and crooks like you."

The easy contempt in his face had at last succeeded in stinging Angelo to anger and he spat out, "The bishop told you himself that the people like me better than the priests," the words were out before Angelo had realized their implication and the two men were left staring at each other.

"If you heard that, you must have heard what I said in reply," said Robert genially. "You remember I said that I would never believe that a gangster could give the people what they wanted. He rules by terror and not by law."

"Get going and keep going," said Angelo.

As Robert walked away he wondered whether he should go back and tell the bishop that Angelo must have had a microphone installed when he had had the bishop's rooms wired for light and power. But out of some inertia, he did not. It didn't seem worth it.

Chapter 9

IT WAS DARK BEFORE GEMMA REACHED HOME AND FOUND THAT her father was out at a town meeting and Robert waiting for her in the upstairs room. He had been trying to see her most of the afternoon, going to and fro between the pharmacy and his room. While he was packing the things he would want for the journey, he had drunk almost a whole bottle of dry Martini and several small glasses of *grappa* without reflecting that they might make him tipsy. Gemma was so late because she had twisted her ankle coming down the mountain and had limped the last few kilometers in great pain. There was something desperate and slatternly in her appearance, like a girl from the slums long past caring, which was due not only to dirt, to pain and to fatigue.

At Robert's words: "I'm going to America tomorrow," she sat down suddenly in a chair, put her hand to her breast, and turning away her head, said, "Don't bother to give explanations."

Robert disregarded the remark and went on, "I haven't much time and I have a heap of things to say to you."

"Don't bother, I know what they are." Gemma gave a sort of deathly grin of despair as she spoke, but still kept her eyes on the carpet. Again Robert ignored her words.

"The first thing is that I'm going back because I have a job of work to do and because I love you. The second is that I shall come back as soon as I possibly can. And the third thing is that I am going to marry you when I get back and I'll live wherever you like: somewhere in Italy or France is my choice. I want you to get those three facts into your head, because I am going away tomorrow and it may be better that I don't write to you."

As Robert spoke Gemma sat up and listened and then looked at him. His fierce, dominating tone was something quite new in their relationship.

"I'm not going to tell you the reasons for my journey in detail. You must accept the fact that it is because of my love for you. One thing I can tell you is that money is involved. There is a trust to be wound up if I am to marry you and settle in Europe and I have to get my half-sister and her lawyer to agree to that." And Robert began to explain the financial affairs of his family.

"I am not much interested. I think I shall go and have a bath." As she walked past him Robert caught her by the wrist and pulled her towards him and kissed her.

132

"I'll come and talk to you while you are having it."

Under some circumstances Gemma would have accepted the suggestion as perfectly natural, but at the moment it irritated her. And she noticed that Robert's breath smelled of alcohol.

"I think you are a bit drunk," she said, stepping away from him. Her tone was harsh, for drunkenness is socially disgraceful among educated Italians. Then an idea struck her and she added, "You've been drinking to keep up your courage. You have made up this story about going to America about money for my sake. I think you are going because you are scared of Angelo over this Ercole business. Once you are gone I shan't see you again."

"How dare you say that! If that's the sort of man you think I am, how could you possibly . . ." Robert almost shouted at her. But Gemma had gone out of the room and as he followed he heard the wards of the lock on the bathroom door click.

The imputation of cowardice is more insulting to an Englishman, or an American than it is to an Italian.

Gemma's words had sobered and cooled Robert. He was too offended, too full of icy reasonable anger to make a scene, and only said through the door:

"I hope you will feel ashamed of saying such cruel things which you know are untrue. I shall be waiting in the dining room when you come out."

133

By the time Gemma had finished her bath she was feeling just a trifle ashamed of herself. She was still furious with Robert for concealing the real motives of his visit to America, for the tone in which he had spoken and the lack of trust which he showed in her. But she was sorry she had accused him of getting drunk because he was afraid, since she thought it was much more likely that his lack of frankness was on her father's advice, or because he was shielding someone whom Ercole was blackmailing.

But she was proud. When she had come back she had meant to swallow her pride. But it was too much for her. What she had said might be true and she delayed the moment when she would go back into the dining room and make up the quarrel with her lover.

The forty minutes of waiting passed easily for Robert, as he picked up a book, and though he was shaking with anger when he opened it, he began to read it carefully and follow the argument put forward.

He was still reading when Lucchesi came in.

"Hasn't Gemma come home yet?" he asked anxiously.

"She's having a bath and sulking because I told her she ought to be ashamed of herself," said Robert.

"What was her offence?"

"She said I had got drunk because I was scared and that I was running away from Angelo to America."

134

Lucchesi laughed and then told Robert that he had thought of a way for him to write to Gemma from America without attracting attention. He was to put his letters into envelopes that he would give him, with the printed business heading of a firm of chemical and drug wholesalers in Milan and send the letter in a covering envelope to the manager who was an old friend to forward. Robert's love letters would thus appear to be part of the business mail and arouse no interest.

"A lot of the postal sorters are Communists and if you wrote frequently Angelo would certainly hear about the letters with American stamps — he might even open one or two of them before delivery."

"In that case I might write one or two bogus letters to lead him astray, telling Gemma, for instance, that there was no hope of my ever coming back to Europe."

Lucchesi was still laughing when Gemma came in. In spite of her pride she had stopped to listen at the door and had overheard what her father and her lover had been saying. So in some way Angelo was involved! She nodded to each of them, but she would not speak to either. After a few minutes, Robert said good night without making any move to kiss her, and went back to his room. He was angry both with her and with himself. He was a fool to be going back to the States. He was going on a fool's errand. The guess that

Angelo had a criminal record there was a wild shot in the dark. Even if it were true it was a thousand to one that he could not prove it.

There was still half a liter of rather poisonous *grappa* left and Robert gulped down a glassful of the fiery stuff. But even so he could not sleep until he had taken two pills of phenobarbital. He could afford to sleep late as his bag was packed and he did not leave San Frediano till midday.

Robert woke with the first light, aware that someone had come into his room. For a few seconds he lay inert, groping for the consciousness and judgment that were required. Then he slid his hand under the bolster and grasped the Steyr automatic that Lucchesi had lent him and turned his head slowly.

It was Gemma. The moment Robert saw her he tried to hide the pistol, but she pounced upon it.

"That is my father's, isn't it? Well, you don't need it for the moment."

She came and sat beside him, and her whole face seemed lit up with love and tenderness. With her soft long fingers she stroked his cheek.

"Your face is too rough," and she kissed him long and passionately on the mouth. "Do you know that I said to myself if he demands an apology before he kisses me, I shall walk out on him forever."

"I haven't had a chance to do either yet," said Robert —

and then took the chance that her astonishment offered.

After that Robert must have blinked or shown he was still only partly awake, for Gemma said, "Go to sleep again and let me do what I like."

Robert lay back and pretended to obey her, but after some minutes passivity became almost unbearable and he tore himself away, and began to make love to her himself.

"How do you come to be here?" he asked at last.

"Signora Salerno leaves her back door unlatched when she goes to Matins."

Gemma was made with the temperament that can love and make love again and again. Indeed, Robert never felt that there was a limit. The waves would retreat over the ribs of sand until all was bare and dry upon the shore and then the waters slowly gathered themselves up trembling in a thousand cross-currents and sweeping him out of his depth, came running in across the sands until they finally broke in a crash of foam and thunder that left him barely struggling for life. Only when he finally lost consciousness, or gave himself up as irretrievably drowned, did the breakers cease and after the uncounted storms and whirlpools did the mariner wake at last to find the warm sun playing upon him and a flat calm upon the sea. For so long as he could ride the surf, the waves ran mountains high.

What recalled him to consciousness — to his second awakening that morning, was hearing Gemma saying through a crack in the door, "Bring us up two breakfasts, Signora Salerno. Coffee, rolls, and honey."

It occurred to Robert then that Gemma had flung away her last shred of reputation in the little town, but it was not until some time later that he asked himself why she had done so. Was it because of her genuine passion and abiding love? Or was it from a longing to make a high and noble end of their love-making and to prove that her own did not count the cost?

When they were drinking their coffee as they lay side by side in bed, Gemma said, "Before you go, I think that you should know about my past love affair. You have never asked. I don't like thinking about it . . . and anyway I wasn't sure that you were interested."

Robert noticed that Gemma was not overcoming shyness, or embarrassment, the strain in her was due to an effort to speak impartially of something about which nobody in the world who had experienced it could be dispassionate.

"I was waiting for you to tell me when you wanted to," he said.

"I thought it might be delicacy which kept you from asking . . . When I was studying music at Milan there was a girl in my class called Bettina. She fell in love with me and I with her. Such things weren't very unusual among the set of girls I mixed with in Milan. I found out later that she had had relations with most of them. Bettina was big and strong and very fair, but with brown eyes: her family were partly Austrian. She was a year younger than I was and infinitely more experienced. I ought to have said that she had a lovely voice, but was not really interested in music — not seriously, I mean. Well, we managed to arrange to share the same room and after that she made love to me every night and I made love to her tirelessly. We were indefatigable . . . and it was a revolution in my life. Everything else went to the winds for those three weeks at the end of the summer term.

"Bettina's family took a house at Cesenatico for the holidays and I went to stay with them. We spent our whole time either in the sea or in each other's arms."

Gemma paused for such a long time that at last Robert said, "Well, go on. Finish your story."

"One day her brother Ludovico came home on leave. He is an officer on a boat trading to Sydney, Australia. Of course it was a great excitement his coming home, but I never even flirted with him. Bettina was everything to me. Then one day he took us both out to dinner and dancing afterwards.

"Ludovico was young, tall, with very fair hair but yellow eyes. He was really extremely handsome, but with thin lips. Bettina and he made me drink a great deal: more than I was used to. After the dance we were very late getting home. Bettina and I went to bed together and I went to sleep at once. When I woke up I was in pain: Ludovico was in bed with me and in the act of raping me. He told me to keep quiet or my reputation would be gone forever; then he swore he had fallen madly in love with me. Finally he told me that he had given Bettina five thousand lire that afternoon to let him take her place. As soon as I was sound asleep she had let him in and gone up to sleep in his bed. She had helped him to make me drink a lot and then had persuaded me to take a pill. She said it would make me sleep sounder and it did.

"The extraordinary thing was that Ludovico's story was true. When I asked Bettina about it next morning she laughed and offered me a share of the money! I was beside myself. I thought that I should die of shame and horror. I went home as soon as I could next morning. Ludovico insisted on coming on the coach and swore he was madly in love with me and told me he would kill me and himself unless I went on seeing him. He actually asked my father for his consent to his marrying me. I ought to have told my father the whole story then — but I didn't and I was idiot enough to get engaged to Ludovico and accept him as my lover. Ten days later he went back to his ship. I found that I was pregnant. I went and stayed with Giovanna, the stonecutter's wife in the mountains and she brought about a miscarriage for me. I went to see her again yesterday . . ."

"If you are pregnant now you must have the child," interrupted Robert.

"No, I'm not, darling. I went to tell her about you and

our quarrel and she said I must swallow my pride and tell you the whole story."

Gemma paused and then making an effort continued in a matter of fact voice, "Ludovico has never written to me once. He was utterly selfish, heartless and corrupt as his sister. I have suffered a great deal from shame . . ." As she said the last words Gemma suddenly broke down and began sobbing. She turned away from Robert burying her face in the pillow.

He did not speak but using all his strength, turned her over in the bed and took her in his arms and then began kissing her very gently and stroking her until the sobs and convulsive movements ceased. At last when she lay silent, he said, "What you have just told me makes it a thousand times harder for me to go away. I want to be with you always. When I come back, I shall never leave you again."

"Nobody knows about the last part of it except the woman on the mountain," said Gemma.

They spoke a little of the future and Gemma said, "Of course I shall be here when you return . . . whenever it is, I shall be here. Or you can send for me to come anywhere and I shall come."

"I rely on you to wait for me. Perhaps only a few weeks, perhaps two or three months." It was time to go to the coach.

They dressed hurriedly. Signora Salerno was in tears at parting.

Gemma said to her, "My father and I will come and fetch away the signore's books and other belongings later on to-day."

It was the unbearable moment before departure, of the realization that in another ten, five, three, two minutes the separation will have taken place: that nothing can stop it, can restore happiness, put time back where it was — that we are all fragile Humpty-Dumpties — we are always being shattered; we can never be put together again; and that at every moment of our lives we are embarking upon the unknown, and never completing what we have begun.

This realization led Robert to say, as Gemma and he walked across the piazza, "Everything will be different when I come back. But my love will be just the same. Nothing could make me love you less."

Gemma had been strained and silent but at this she burst out laughing.

"Oh, dearest Robert! You angel! What a glorious declaration of passion. 'Nothing can make me love you less!' It doesn't sound right, does it? Nothing, except your saying that, at this moment, could ever make me love you more."

Gemma had not often shown her sense of humor before; but it seemed delightful to be laughed at just then: her laughter was more intimate than tears could ever be, and was a good augury for the future.

The conductor put Robert's suitcase in the baggage compartment and Gemma led him aside and then kissed him while the coach-load of passengers waited and the conductor gossiped with the driver and the last seconds during which they could hold each other ticked away.

And then, at the last possible moment, Lucchesi appeared, having apparently materialized, a little out of breath, through the surface of the concrete of the coach station — which nobody had noticed him crossing. He walked up to Robert, took him by the hand, and after shaking it warmly, kissed him rather solemnly on each cheek. Robert knew that Lucchesi would never have dreamed of kissing him except in public, and that the act was in the nature of a formal benediction and acknowledgment. Any scandal that the good-natured Signora Salerno might spread with regard to Gemma, would lose much of its savor thanks to the mayor's public embrace of his daughter's departing lover.

But suddenly Robert realized that the little man was in a state of considerable emotion. He was blinking his eyes and behind one of the thick lenses a magnified tear was trembling on the lower lid.

"Don't stay away long, my dearest son. We shall both be very unhappy until your return." He squeezed Robert's hand convulsively, several tears dropped and to cover this, he fished about in his coat pocket and pulled out a packet of Kwells.

"Take one an hour before you start and you won't be seasick. They actually do work."

The conductor was standing at the mayor's elbow. Robert kissed Gemma for the last time, boarded the bus, and almost before he had taken his seat, they had passed through the old gateway and were rushing at high speed towards the first of the hairpin bends in the road which led down the foothills into the plain of the Romagna.

Chapter 10

Robert's visit to washington was a fiasco. as the friends he had been counting on had gone on a holiday to Mexico and he knew absolutely nobody else, he spent a week alone. There was nobody to give him the personal introduction to the F.B.I. which he knew was necessary; however, he wrote in, outlining his suspicions and asking if they had any information on Angelo in their files.

This brought him a call from two elegantly dressed officers in plain clothes. The spokesman was a tall good-looking man, about forty, with gray hair, cut short, gray eyes, wearing a well-cut gray suit and brown suède shoes. His companion was a little younger, not quite so tall, not quite so obviously a gentleman, but good-looking, with blue eyes and a well-cut blue suit. Robert took them up to his bedroom and offered them cigarettes, which they accepted, and drinks, which they declined. He gave them Lucchesi's notes, the photographs of Angelo, the fingerprints and explained why he had become suspicious. But he soon saw that they were more interested in him than in Angelo. They asked him with perfect politeness why he had been staying in San Frediano and seemed to think his explanations unconvincing, though they were too polite to say so outright. His book aroused polite but persistent interest. How long did he propose to live in Europe if he returned there? Why had he been for so long absent from America? Before leaving they took possession of his passport and asked him for a banker's reference.

Robert was furious — for it was clear that he had got nowhere and that he was wasting his time. Next day he took the plane to New York to consult his lawyer.

In New York he had friends: if the city was not his home exactly, he knew his way around and could enjoy himself. Everyone he met seemed to expect him to think that it had changed out of recognition because the El had gone and there were a lot of new buildings. But change was the essential quality of New York; if there had been none, its whole spirit would have been unrecognizable. Just because of the changes the essential character of the city was the same. It was big; it was glorious; it was free. It was a triumphant city, and it would go on to greater triumphs.

In Europe he had hated the idea of seeing Caroline's brother, here it seemed positively delightful. Perhaps nothing was a better illustration of the different state of mind which New York imposed.

In any case it was the sensible thing to do. Colonel Stephenson would be friendly; he could bear witness that he had originally suggested that Robert should stay in San Frediano. It would be a relief to meet someone who could talk about the little town and who knew Gemma and her father. It was possible also that Stephenson, who was on a military mission to the United States, might know some influential officer who could straighten out the tangle in which he seemed to have got himself with the F.B.I.

Ten minutes after telephoning, Robert found himself being warmly greeted by Caroline's brother in his New York office.

Patrick Stephenson looked like a character out a novel by Anthony Hope or Elinor Glyn — the irresistible hero, or the madly attractive villain. One guessed immediately (but wrongly) that he carried a swordstick and one anticipated the clash of steel on steel. He was tall, emaciated, dark and strikingly handsome, with gay, dancing black eyes, an aquiline nose and cruel lips, which were, however, always smiling. He was wearing a Brigade of Guards tie and was immaculately dressed and obviously took some pains to be so. Robert simply could not begin to imagine him hiding in a mountain cave with Lucchesi. It was unthinkable that he should ever be unshaved, or his boots unpolished.

Everyone else whom Robert had seen in America had appeared either exhausted, or caught up in a whirlwind of engagements, or both. Patrick Stephenson seemed to have infinite leisure and not a care in the world.

"How do you like being back?"

"I'm hating it."

"Oh, I love America. I wouldn't live anywhere else in the world. It's a heavenly country; enchanting people," said the colonel, clasping his carefully manicured thin hands behind his head and laughing. "Why, I never knew what life was until I came here. What's wrong? Why do you hate it?"

He listened carefully and the smile disappeared as Robert sketched the reasons that had brought him to America and described his misadventures in Washington.

"I expect I can straighten that out for you; come up to my place in Connecticut for the week end. I'll drive you up tomorrow."

Robert accepted and went on to see his lawyer greatly cheered and confident.

But that evening he was asking himself why he had been such a fool as to accept. Did Colonel Stephenson know that he had been his sister's lover? Did he know anything about Caroline? And could he himself be sure that a week end spent in her brother's company would not start everything again and send him out of his wits?

*   *   *

Through the window of the little top room in College Street Robert would catch sight of Caroline for a moment or two before she crossed to his side of the gleaming wet street and vanished under the parapet. She had the key of the street door but he could not hear her open or close it, or the sound of her feet on the stairs, and there was no noise as she pushed open the door of his room, no sound until she sighed deeply and dropped her parcels, bag, coat, with rain on the fur, scarf and hat, in the body of the armchair, before she came up to him and let him take her in his arms. Her eyes were so soft and so dark as he kissed her. She did not want — would not let him speak. She put her hand on his mouth at his first words. Then as he stood beside her, she would silently take off her clothes and slip into bed and he would hurriedly do the same. Her touch was gentle and sent shivers chasing up his spine; her body was as soft as an owl's wing.

It was always four o'clock in the afternoon and when Big Ben struck five, she would remove his hand from where it rested, smile at him, and getting out of bed, sit down in front of the hissing gas fire and warm her clothes before putting each of them on. She would not allow him to speak. When he begged her to stay the night, to meet him for dinner, to come to Paris, to live with him, to marry him, she said, "No. All that's impossible. I shan't come again if you make scenes. Let's stay like this."

He lay naked on the bed until she had gone and if he had refrained from speaking, telling her of his love and asking her to marry him, she would give him a last strange soft kiss, brushing his body with her fur coat and she would say, "Oh, you can. You can! No one can better!"

Her eyes had been bright and cruel when she had told him at the beginning that no one must know of her liaison with him. He must never go to houses where he might meet her. If they met by chance — in the street, at a theater, in a restaurant, he must not dare to lift his hat, he must understand that she would cut him dead. He must never try to find out anything more than he already knew about her.

He knew a good deal. She lived in a house in South Kensington with Lady Savage, who was separated from her husband. Lord Savage farmed in Kenya and their grown-up daughter was married and trained horses at Newmarket.

Though she would not let Robert speak of his love for her, Caroline would sometimes say to him, "Oh, thank you, my lover. Oh, my lover." Robert believed that Caroline must love him. But why, if she did, this mystery? Why this ruthless doing violence to all the lover's instinct to share the life of and cherish the beloved? How could he be sure of anything? How live the other twenty-three hours of each day?

Many men might have asked nothing better than what Caroline gave him, but Robert Harcourt, being what he was, went almost insane with agitation. Love could not be only the exchanges of the body, or even that momentary sharing and communion of the spirit which those exchanges brought. Love was living together, companionship, unbroken intimacy, children. But when he told her that, her forehead would wrinkle in a frown, her eyes grow hard and bright and she would say, "Do you mean to drive me away forever? Why can't you be happy with what I give you?" And then if he spoke again she would put her hand over his mouth.

All that first winter Caroline came to his room three or four times a week. Then in the spring she stopped coming. The sparrows were tearing the crocuses to pieces in Kensington Gardens. There was an east wind; his skin was tight and dry and in spite of an occasional sharp pain in his chest he felt disembodied as though he were a piece of dirty paper blowing along over the grass, when, seeing her coming at last towards him, he rose from the seat where he had been waiting and moved towards her. He had no idea what he had said, but she had listened.

"You look as though you were ill; go back to your room and go to bed. I'll try to come on Tuesday." She walked as far as the Serpentine with him, then stopped a cab, told him to get in, gave the driver his address and slammed the door. He did not see or hear of her for three months. He was in bed for six weeks with pneumonia and when he was convalescing Lady Savage's Austrian cook kept telling him that Miss Stephenson was out of town, had gone for a long visit to the country, or even that she was abroad.

And then, and then and then. Why think about her any more?

∗   ∗   ∗

It was madness to have accepted Patrick Stephenson's invitation. It just showed how far he had escaped from Caroline — and it would be intolerable to be reminded of her, impossible not to think of her. All the time that he was going to be in Patrick's company he would be thinking so vividly of Caroline, soft as an owl's wing, and of Caroline sitting warming her garments in front of the gas fire before she put them on, that it would be impossible for Patrick not to see the images that were in his mind.

That night Robert was unable to sleep until he had taken two phenobarbital pills. But when he woke Caroline had retreated far into the past. At breakfast there was a letter forwarded from San Frediano. He did not recognize the handwriting and was surprised when he read:

CARISSIMO ROBERTO:

This is a begging letter: so let us get the unpleasant part over at once. Owing to the truly Machiavellian machinations of that abominable scoundrel Angelo — and owing to that clever trick played on me by a dear friend whom I will not name, I am now entirely destitute and forced to live on the charity of my friends. I dislike it as both the charity and the friendship are practically nonexistent.

I have served Angelo's turn and now that I no longer have the negatives, which I always refused to let him see, I am useless to him. He whitewashes himself by blackguarding me to everyone in San Frediano and when I asked him

152

for a loan he threatened to denounce me to the police, or to have me shut up in an asylum for what he calls my "perverse tastes." Damn it all, I am just a working photographer and I took immense pains to get the pictures Angelo wanted — indeed I got my bottom kicked and only escaped a horse-whipping by a miracle of agility.

As you can imagine I don't like the profession of beggar. It is ghastly spending so much money on stationery and stamps and nerve-wracking waiting for letters one *positively knows* will never come. But I am destitute, having pawned my lovely Leica. I have, however, a brilliant future before me — as I have been offered the job of reporter and photographer to a new weekly called the *Eavesdropper* which is being launched here to advertise "What's On" in three Northern Italian Cities, also photographs of leading hostesses, girls on the marriage market, etc. Then a sparkling gossip column and photographs of distinguished visitors to our towns. I am due to provide pictures for the first number which comes out in two months' time. No one in the photographic, or optical trade will trust me with the loan of a camera. I owe all of them money and daren't go into the shops. If I can't get my Leica out of pawn in the next fortnight I shall have to nerve myself to murder an American soldier on leave, choosing the smallest man with the largest camera. But I have not the right temperament for an assassin.

Reflect that if you send me fifty thousand lire now, it will prove an immense economy for you, as I should otherwise be borrowing fifteen thousand every month. Moreover, if I keep the job, if I keep straight, if I turn over an entirely new leaf, it would be wonderful to pay you the money back! Would not that be astonishing? It gives me a kick to think of the day when I do that. Not that I believe it will ever come.

I embrace you — my dearest — and only American friend.

Your affectionate
ERCOLE.

P.S. If you refuse me now, I shall take advantage of your bad conscience and pester you till I die. My cries for help will go unanswered, I suppose. But think of the awful day when the usual monthly begging letter doesn't arrive! After a week without sleep you will go to the morgue and you will see, lying on the marble slab, with his toenails uncut, his denture falling out and his ribs sticking through his skin, this whoreson scoundrel Ercole . . . which gives me a new idea. Could I raise the money on the promise of delivering my carcass after death to an unscrupulous maker of *mortadella* sausage? He wouldn't have long to wait. If I pull this off, I'll get him to post a slice to all my friends and relations (it would let him in for about five and a half slices) — each packed in a little box like wedding cake but with a mourning band round it. If I remember, such an arrangement is called a *post obit;* but I don't suppose you know Latin. Yours till the morgue or the *mortadella!*

The idea that Ercole should expect him to help get his camera out of hock made Robert grin, and he laughed at al-

154

most every line in the letter. There was no guarantee that Ercole would not start work for Angelo again, except that San Frediano was now too hot to hold him. It was more likely that he would set up as a free-lance blackmailer on his own. Indeed the *Eavesdropper* sounded a promising springboard for such activities.

Robert's lawyer had handed him a check on account of the trust settlement of five thousand dollars. Ercole's begging letter could not have been better timed. Robert put five twenty-dollar notes between a sheet of blotting paper in an envelope and sent it by air mail. If Ercole got in trouble with the police it would be difficult for them to trace the gift back to him.

That afternoon Colonel Stephenson drove Robert from New York to his country house in Connecticut, along the Parkway, its forest verges still radiant in the red and gold of autumn. For nearly a hundred miles Robert was astonished by the beauty of America and still more astonished to find the word "civilized" continually coming to his lips.

The Parkway with its dual carriageways, carefully tended verges, undisfigured by a single advertisement and undefiled by litter, was far more civilized than any road in Italy, or for that matter, in Europe.

Robert felt a glow of pleasure at being an American, just as he had done in New York.

The paradoxical feature was that the Englishman, Patrick

Stephenson seemed to take Robert's eulogies personally, and to be delighted to show off New England to an appreciative stranger.

"But of course. Our little communities in New England are more highly civilized than anywhere in the world."

Colonel Stephenson's white clapboard house was half hidden by tall oaks and looked out over a stream that swelled to a woodland pool. It was silent and restful, without a house in sight. But as soon as they had pulled open the outer screen door and pushed through the inner door into the dining room, all thoughts of the perfections of the New World were banished.

"I'm afraid I've sair news for both of you," said the Scottish housekeeper, handing Robert a piece of paper on which she had written down a cable which had been telephoned from New York half an hour before. It read: FATHER DIED THIS MORNING. GEMMA.

Robert handed it to Patrick.

"I must fly back," he said.

"I wonder if you should. But you haven't got your passport back, have you? I must get busy on that."

"Gemma is alone and she will need me. I am certain that Angelo is responsible for this. If you can help me to get my passport, I can be back there in twenty-four hours."

"I don't think I can do anything till Monday."

Robert pushed open the door and went out. He wanted to be alone.

The sun was throwing a long shadow over the little lake, but the birch trees, scattered among the oaks and maples, shone white-limbed dryads in the last rays. Suddenly Robert reflected that once the funeral was over and the shop let or sold, Gemma was no longer tied to San Frediano. They could marry and live wherever they felt inclined: in New England if they chose. He need no longer bother about Angelo. A weight was lifted from his shoulders. A distaste for his researches had been growing. Robert was not afraid of Angelo. He thought it very possible that when he went back to San Frediano the fellow would try and get him bumped off — why shouldn't he? The old French quip: *"Cet animal est méchant: quand on l'attaque, il se defend,"* seemed to meet the case. Robert did not feel fear. He felt a heavy weight of antipathy to what was almost bound to develop: violence, or threats of violence, calling in the police, affidavits before public notaries, the law. What would it all be in aid of, now that Lucchesi was dead? Revenge was utterly pointless and so was punishment. There were bound to be gangsters who became Communist politicians. It was in the natural order of things. Why should he bother about one more? Angelo was certainly by no means the worst of them. Robert remembered the clever suggestion of blackmail, the shabby treatment of poor Ercole when he had served his turn. Such things were common enough in political life. Now he must go back and talk to Patrick and see how soon he could arrange to fly back to Italy. There were other guests coming for the week end. He must try to conceal his agitation. If only he could get away before they came.

There was a car by the house when he returned: American voices, introductions awaiting him — and the welcome question: "Scotch or bourbon?"

And there was Patrick, casually interrupting the chatter of his guests, while he poured the whisky over the ice, with the words, "I've solved our problems while you were down by the lake, Harcourt. First I telegraphed to Caroline, who luckily is in Rome, to go and look after Gemma. You remember, of course, that she knows her. That gives you time to decide what you will do. Then I've fixed it so that you'll get your passport back by the end of the week."

Robert took the glass mechanically.

"Do you think Caroline will go?" he asked.

"Of course. She'll be there tomorrow. You'll find her there when you get back . . . and you needn't go back until you want to."

Oh, bright-eyed, cruel-mouthed, elegant incomprehension! Oh, disaster piled upon disaster! Robert drank off the whisky and held out the glass piled up with ice and Patrick at least had the humanity to fill it up again immediately.

"So you have only just come home from Italy, Mr. Harcourt?" asked a slim young woman.

That week end Robert thought more about Caroline than he had done since his first week at San Frediano. He kept going over the past and speculating anxiously about the future. Lucchesi's death seemed also strangely unreal; he could not realize that he would never see him again, or imagine the little town without him.

* * *

And then, and then, and then, after Robert had recovered from pneumonia, maddeningly silly that had been, defying all the prohibitions, he had scraped acquaintance with Lady Savage and soon got to know her well enough to be always welcome at her house. Had he guessed her secret? Did she guess his?

Pink-cheeked and bright-eyed, the cruel lips bent in a smile, Caroline arrived back every evening in time to dispense drinks and to greet Charlie, Pablo and Robert himself with friendly amusement.

Where, with whom had she been from four to five that afternoon? Lady Savage, with hooded eyes and Lesbian bonhomie, did not ask. She liked having men about the place, enjoyed teasing Pablo the sleepy Peruvian, and liked to tell Robert stories about her husband and life in Kenya.

"I left him when the Mau Mau started. I'm a fearful coward and I couldn't stand waiting for the black boys one had liked and had trusted to come and chop one in pieces with their *pangas* — their bush knives. No, I couldn't stand that. Now Caroline's brave, like her brother. She wouldn't have minded a bit, would you Caroline?"

"Have some more gin and French," said Caroline, taking Robert's glass.

"Mau Mau was rather a blessing in disguise for me, if you know what I mean. I had had as much as I could stand of married life and Africa," said Lady Savage.

Oh, those hours of corroding jealousy when he came away from the deathly house in South Kensington, in that soul-destroying neighborhood of Cromwell Road. The savage repentance of his own folly! Why had he not kept Caroline upon her own terms? What more could a man want, than what she had given him? To have thrown away, smashed up, forfeited happiness because like the fool in a fairy story he had looked for more than was permitted. How often he had said to himself in those days, "Never, never shall I be such a fool again!" How often told himself that in love one must snatch the joy as it flies. Risk nothing and take what one can. "None but the brave deserves the fair!" And the brave man is he with the strength of mind to dominate a woman and never commit himself to her entirely! But how idiotic all such ideas had been! In Florence he had escaped forever from Caroline's poison. And now Caroline was with Gemma, and she would poison her, as once she had poisoned him.

"Oh, my God! Am I being too silly? Am I being romantic? I can't tell. But it was madness and folly ever to have left Gemma." And then, and then, and then.

* * *

Robert wondered whether Caroline had got bored and had broken off with Lady Savage. He guessed that anyway she would have been left behind in Rome, if not in Kensington. Possibly it would simplify things if she had gone to San Frediano also. It would limit Caroline's opportunities for mischief. The sooner that he went back himself the better.

The day after his return to New York, Robert received an air mail letter from Gemma, written before her cable.

CARISSIMO,

I haven't written because I am a good deal worried, and have waited hoping to send good news. But it isn't really very good. Papa was found unconscious in the shop three days ago. Apparently he had had a stroke, or had fainted, and in falling had hit his head and lost a great deal of blood. It was altogether very mysterious. He has been unconscious almost ever since, but he rallied this morning and said: "Tell him to be careful. He must be careful."

That was all. But I am sure he meant you. I am writing

in his room and have been with him all the time. Everyone is very kind and good. I'm sorry but I can't write more. Do come back soon.

GEMMA

Next morning there was another letter:

DEAREST,

You will have got my telegram. There is nothing to say. He was lying unconscious for a week during which I slept in the same room at night and scarcely left him during the day. It was, they say, without any possible doubt caused by a heart attack or sudden fainting fit and when he fell he hit his temple on the brass stopcock which turns off the water to the sink behind the counter. This has been proved, and I tell you in case you are imagining all sorts of melodramas and acts of foul play.

Somehow it's being an accident makes it worse and more meaningless and there is nothing to do but weep and wring one's hands. He and I were one. He was entirely unselfish, entirely good; never swayed in his judgment by personal advantage.

The professor of whom I told you, came from Pisa and spoke, at the side of the grave, of Father's heroic leadership and personal bravery as a commandant of the partisans. He said also, which pleased me very much, that Father was the most completely intellectual and humane man whom he had known, entirely free from prejudice and superstition and that it was a loss to Italy that he had not qualified in medicine or taught in a University.

162

Dearest, I love you all the more because he loved you, and it was of you he was thinking during the few moments when he recovered consciousness. And I send all my love to Colonel Stephenson, who fought beside him against the Fascists and the Germans. I seem to have forgotten how to sleep and I am ten years older than when you went away. Nothing is worth while now. I am very lonely, but there are fortunately still things to be done. I have to engage a manager for the shop; otherwise I should beat my head against the wall.

I don't see why you shouldn't come back. Surely you have settled the legal business with your sister by now?

Love and kisses,
GEMMA

Robert felt that he must get back as soon as possible. But he was unable to do so. As soon as the legal formalities were completed, he went down with another attack of pneumonia, his second within a year, while he was staying with his sister in Vermont. He was rushed to the nearest hospital, and his recovery was slow. Gemma wrote once or twice, saying very little. He was still only allowed up for an hour or two every afternoon when he received a letter from her that aroused his worst suspicions of Caroline.

DEAREST ROBERT,

Do take care of yourself. Otherwise I would say: Come back as soon as you possibly can, though I have been told that that is what I must not say. I don't know what I really feel, or where I am since Father died and since Caroline has been here. She is wonderfully kind to me and I think without her, or you, I should have gone mad. But perhaps I am a little mad. Caroline is a strange person. She is jealous of you and doesn't like me to write, although I am not allowed to be jealous of all the others. I am writing this in secret and posting it myself. Everyone is in love with her: all the girls and women, and there is something recently between her and Angelo that I don't completely understand. I love her terribly and she makes me very happy sometimes. But you see I love you as much as ever, Robert, in spite of her because I am writing like this. Dearest Robert, I don't know what will happen to us, but when we see each other we shall know better and shall be able to arrange things. Come back as soon as it is safe for you to travel.

Love and kisses from
GEMMA

The day after he received this letter, Robert insisted on leaving the hospital in spite of the protests of the doctor in charge of his case, said good-by to his sister and took the train to New York.

It no longer mattered that he had failed to find out anything about Angelo. But when he took Patrick Stephenson out to lunch and mentioned his failure, the Englishman said, "I feel sure that you went to the wrong people. You assumed that Angelo was a gangster in America. So you went to the F.B.I. But suppose he were a U.S. soldier who had shot his superior officer and had then deserted?"

"I suppose that is perfectly possible," said Robert. "But wouldn't the F.B.I. be after him?"

"Not if it happened during the war and in Europe, and he deserted and got away. That would fit all the facts you know. But the record would be in the U. S. Army files. If you'll give me the papers I'll have his record looked up — if he has one. But there is absolutely no point in your staying here. If they find that Angelo has a criminal record and that he is an American citizen, they won't tell you or me. They will go right ahead with the Italian Government, possibly on a high level, possibly ordinary extradition. But you won't know anything about it until Angelo is suddenly arrested."

So much for Angelo. There was a pause while the waiter brought their steaks. Then Robert asked:

"Did you ever meet the wife of a stonecutter in the 'high mountain' called Giovanna?"

At this unexpected question the spick-and-span Englishman, always apparently master of himself, seemed embarrassed and blushed.

"Yes, I stayed three weeks with her. I was wounded and got a complication of fever and food poisoning on top of that. Really she saved my life and I may as well tell you that I fell in love with her. It was a strange experience."

165

"What is she like?"

"In 1944 she was a woman of about forty: still very handsome with a girl's figure. Immensely strong. She has natural authority. There are only a few quarrymen and shepherds up there and she keeps them in complete submission. But Gemma must have told you about her?"

"Very little, except that her father took her up there after her mother was murdered, and that Giovanna looked after her till some months after the war was over."

There was a pause. Patrick Stephenson seemed to be looking for words.

"Giovanna has never been educated, but she has taught herself to speak correct Italian and to read and write it. The Italians are an intelligent race and she struck me as the most intelligent Italian I have ever met. She seemed to be able to understand anything — I mean anything — if I explained it once or twice."

"Don't they have odd beliefs up there?" asked Robert.

"Didn't Gemma tell you that Giovanna used to be a witch? I mean a real thorough-going witch, with power over animals, familiars, flying by night, brewing potions, everything?"

"How much do you believe?"

"Nothing at all, naturally. I'm not a shepherd living in the Appenines. If you press me hard I would admit that she may have some kind of hypnotic powers of an unusual kind.

But they weren't required in my case. I was convalescent and she was a very handsome woman in close physical contact with me. It doesn't need magic philters and love potions to make a wounded soldier fall in love with his nurse."

Robert laughed. "So she didn't convert you to witchcraft?"

"It was rather the other way. I gave her ideas which shook her faith in the supernatural. But I made the mistake of taking Caroline to see her after the war when I went to visit Lucchesi. After we had been there an hour she told me that Caroline was evil and that she wouldn't let her stay. I had to bring her down the mountain at once. We lost our way in the dark and had to sleep in a haybarn."

"How do you account for Giovanna's behavior?"

"I think it was pure jealousy — the jealousy of one powerful and beautiful woman for another. I think she was jealous of Caroline's influence over me and of her talking all the time to me in a language she did not understand. She is after all a savage and fairly primitive in her habits, so it is natural she should be violently jealous of a beautiful woman with a civilized background."

"Yes, I can understand that. Gemma still sees her and asks her advice. When she was very angry with me, she went up the mountain and Giovanna told her to swallow her pride and make it up."

"She thinks of Gemma as her child; she cares about her

happiness and is proud of her being a civilized woman. It's quite different from meeting Caroline," said Stephenson.

"Gemma is wildly romantic about all the primitive religion and witch-cult business," said Robert.

"I don't think it's only romanticism. I think it's a genuine streak of paganism which has developed owing to her love and respect for Giovanna. I can quite understand it." Patrick Stephenson smiled, and drank off the last of his whisky. "But I prefer America." He paused and added, "However, you are going back to Italy, and if you want to be happy with Gemma, I strongly advise you to get Giovanna on your side."

Robert handed the papers about Angelo to Colonel Stephenson and flew back that night.

Chapter II

It was ten o'clock at night when robert reached san Frediano. He drove straight to Signora Salerno's where he had taken his room again, left his bag there and then, although he was dropping with fatigue, walked across the piazza and down the hill to the Lucchesi shop. The moon had just risen. The arcades in light and shadow were like a backcloth on the stage. The side door was ajar and there were many voices in the room above: eager disputing and noisy laughter. Then before he had time to ring the bell, came the sound of the violin and of a piano accompaniment. What was the piece? Perhaps Corelli. Robert waited, propping himself against the wall, for its conclusion then, when the voices were beginning again, rang long and loudly. No notice was taken. He put his finger on the button and kept it there.

The door opened and Gemma stepped out wearing a plain, closely fitting black dress. The longed-for embrace;

the first raptures! Yes. They were there. But was it possible that all the time Gemma was aware of an audience waiting for her reappearance just behind her in the room? She was shining-eyed, kissing him and holding him close. Yet she drew him back too soon into the lighted room to exhibit him and turning, called aloud, "Caroline, Roberto is here; he has flown from America."

There were half a dozen other people in the room. Caroline was on the piano stool. Robert looked away. A young man, dark and handsome, whom he had not seen before, the doctor's two daughters, an unknown woman, Angelo and his wife. What could have induced that bat out of hell to make an appearance? And why should Gemma have invited that son of a bitch, who, in spite of what they all said, was quite possibly responsible for her father's death? How had the enemy got within the fort?

But Robert had no time to ask himself questions or to follow a line of thought. Caroline was upon him. Her lips were fuller but her mouth was crueler than her brother's; her eyes bright with the excitement of welcome and exaggerated surprise. "Oh, Robert, what a surprise! We thought you were still in New York." But he had cabled. Then, just to surprise him, since he had so surprised her, a cheek was held out for him to kiss, then hands gripping both of his, eyes so bright, diving into his soul, cheeks coloring swiftly and a warm, long kiss upon the mouth. She was laughing.

"It's such a long time since I've kissed you like that!"

She was dressed in a lovely brown and yellow cut velvet and silk dress with her magnificent shoulders bare.

"How beautiful you are and what a lovely dress," he began, but she was exclaiming about him.

"You're much older, Robert. And ever so much more distinguished!"

"I'm a bit tired. I didn't get much sleep on the plane last night."

He would have liked a drink with a kick in it, but he was in abstemious Italy and there was only the sweet golden wine of San Frediano to drink.

Angelo was watching him very closely. His wife ignored him.

"So you've been in the States, brother?"

"Left New York last night," said Robert.

"Did you do all you wanted?"

"That would be telling." And Robert laughed.

Gemma introduced him to the young man who had taken over the management of the shop downstairs. The new manager's wife was the neat, shy girl talking to the doctor's elder daughter Emilia. Robert sat down and for a little while let the conversation flow over him. He would have to pick up on the situations which had developed in his absence some other time. Meanwhile he felt resentful that Gemma should not have been alone to greet him when he had got back. After all he had cabled before he left New York.

It seemed that they were all talking, in the way Italians do, endlessly embroidering on the details of a theme, about some incident which had happened in which Caroline had been involved with Father Mangoni. After a bit Robert roused himself to ask her in English what it was.

Caroline moved over to sit next him and replying in English, began telling him that she had gone about a fortnight ago to see the Veroneses in the palace and that finding the door open she had gone in.

"I had been walking round looking at the paintings in the chapel for ten minutes when a horrible young priest rushed up hissing at me and making a lot of rude remarks. I started to go, but he got more and more hysterical and began prodding my arms and shoulders with his fingers and scratching me with his dirty nails. He got into an extraordinary condition; there was foam on his lips and his eyes were popping out of his head. I think he was on the point of having a seizure. It was a frightful scene. Then when I got out of the door on to the staircase, he followed me, still prodding. That was too much, so I turned round and gave him a very hard box on the ear.

"I don't know what would have happened then, if Mr. Angelo hadn't run up the stairs and driven him off. He lived up to his name. Was positively angelic, took me downstairs, gave me a drink and I spent an hour or more making friends with him."

"I suppose that's why he's here."

"Yes — of course. Why shouldn't he be? Look close and you'll see my shoulders are still scratched and bruised."

Caroline rose and inviting Robert to follow her walked to the standard lamp at the other end of the room and turned her back, looking at Robert over her shoulder. He could see one or two faint scratches from Father Mangoni's nails still showing on her creamy white shoulder and the half-twisted golden neck and he smelt the perfume of her body and saw the little dark gold hairs running together to meet the mass of dark brown curls above. And Caroline was laughing back at him provocatively over her shoulder.

But there was Gemma standing beside them with something disturbed and strange in her expression. Robert took hold of her hand and said, "Caroline has been telling me how Angelo rescued her from Father Mangoni."

"That's why she asked Angelo and his wife. It is difficult to explain — but she has made friends with him," said Gemma.

"She began to tell me," said Robert.

"Yes. You understand." Then dismissing the subject Gemma said, "You will sleep here tonight. You will live here with us now."

"I left my bag at Signora Salerno's, before I walked over."

But Gemma stamped her foot. "That is impossible; that is out of the question. It is unheard of. It is insulting! Caroline, Robert is going to live with us now, I insist. You must tell him so, too. Tell him that you want him to stay with us, too."

Caroline laughed. "Of course, Robert. What else?"

Uneasily the three of them walked back to join the others.

Again Robert let the stream of Italian conversation flow over him, lying back to rest in the long chair, drinking the too-sweet golden wine, then filling his glass again and again, and watching Angelo. The handsome face was strained and serious, the green eyes were roaming round the room all the time. He looked profoundly uneasy. Robert guessed that his sudden unexpected arrival had greatly disturbed him; that he wondered if he had fallen into a trap laid for him outside, and was asking himself whether the invitation that evening which had seemed so impromptu and so innocent were part of a carefully laid plan to decoy him from his fortress and to catch him unarmed. But probably he never was and he was reflecting that they would find out their mistake. Had it occurred to him that while he was sitting by the fire listening to Emilia and her sister talking nonsense, his rooms in the palace might be being raided or that the car in which Robert Harcourt had reached San Frediano might have been packed with *carabinieri?*

Robert's speculations had reached that point when Angelo rose uneasily and tapped his wife on the shoulder. "Be moving. Hump yourself."

The departure of the Angelos was the signal for the break-up of the party. The silent manager and his pretty wife were actually the first to go.

"Look at the moon," cried Caroline. "We'll see Bianca and Emilia home, Gemma. Then let's go for a ramble in the moonlight."

"That would be lovely," replied Gemma. "Of course Robert will come with us."

It did not seem to occur to Gemma that Robert must be dog-tired after over twenty-four hours in the air and that he must be longing to be in bed — if possible with her, but at all events stretched between clean sheets, instead of struggling along a mule track after midnight in the moonlight. Or was it a last desperate postponement of a difficult situation — which she had imposed upon the three of them by her insistence that he should sleep in the same house as Caroline and herself? At that moment Robert did not care; any emotional problems would have to be left until the morrow. His job at the moment was to show himself game for whatever was proposed.

"Good night, Signor Angelo. We're going for a walk round the mountain in the moonlight," called Caroline. "Good night, Mrs. Angelo."

"I'll be seeing you," said Angelo. His wife said nothing.

The door slammed and the V-8 roared away up the hill and across the piazza and up the lane to the palace on the hill. Robert was tottering with fatigue, but stepping into the cold night air revived him. He was a new man ready for anything that might come.

They waited while Caroline put on outdoor shoes and pulled her dress up through the silver girdle Robert had given her a year before, until it was knee length with an upper layer falling over like a Greek tunic. Then to Robert's surprise, Emilia and Bianca said they would come with them. Gemma and Caroline led the way out of the town, and almost at once branched off the road. The way was stony and it was easy to stumble. Several times Emilia put her hand out for Robert's help. There were clouds in the sky; suddenly the moon was obscured, the track they were following vanished. The trees in the orchards at the side, and the two figures in front, became invisible. There was Emilia or was it Bianca, groping for Robert, clinging close to him, trembling, breathing into his face, sighing. But it was not what for the first moment he had imagined.

"How lovely Caroline is! She put her hand on my shoulder yesterday and it felt as though I had been burned," said Emilia.

"But Gemma won't let her out of her sight. I should have

thought she and you would have something to say to each other," said Bianca.

"Caroline has been so wonderful with Gemma. I don't know what the poor creature would have done without her, after her father's death. But now she clings; really it's a good thing that you came back when you did," said Emilia.

"Emilia is really just as bad over Caroline as Gemma. I'm a mere looker-on — but I can sympathize with everyone," said Bianca, squeezing Robert's hand.

"That's very sweet of you," said Robert, but soon afterwards he called out to Gemma to wait, and anxious to disentangle himself he said, "I'll help you to find the way."

Then, pushing himself forward, he left Emilia to join her idol and Bianca to waste her sympathy on the night air.

"Where are you taking us?" he asked Gemma.

"The path used to go over this field," she replied drily and he could see that she was ruffled by his masculine assumption of being the natural pathfinder. They struck upwards across a field thickly spread with farmyard manure which was slippery under their shoes. There was a little farmhouse not far away and as they came up to it, a watchdog sprang out barking and almost choking itself in fury. Gemma and Robert recoiled from the animal but the first detour was insufficient, for as they stumbled along away from the track, the dog, beside itself with rage, followed them almost strangling itself in its efforts to attack. Its chain had been fastened round a long wire which left it free to rush up and down the pathway leading to the farm. And it seemed to Robert that the dog's rage was focussed upon him. It was he, the man among the party that it wanted to spring upon and kill. There, with her bare shoulders gleaming in the moonlight and her Grecian tunic, was Caroline transformed into Artemis, there were her two female attendants perhaps ready to tear him to pieces at a word from her, and he himself was Actaeon. If the wire broke, or if the chain became unfastened, he would have to fight off the dog with his bare hands and might be torn to pieces in front of Diana and her attendants.

He wondered for a moment if Gemma saw the dramatic symbolism of the situation. As they left dog and farmhouse behind, a window opened and an angry voice called out in question. Gemma made no reply and called gently, warning Emilia and Bianca to say nothing. They pushed on across another field, but suddenly the moon was obscured again and they were left in darkness.

"Really I don't know where we are," said Gemma. Then turning to Robert she said, half jeering and half affectionate, "You are the man here; you find the way for us."

"All right," said Robert, who was too tired to recognize the flirtatiousness in her words and took them as a challenge. "It's easy enough to find the way. If we go back to the farm, there must be a path leading down from it to the road."

The moon came out and they could see the path and so they cut across to it without going right back to the barking dog and the buildings. But again the dog nearly strangled itself, again the window opened and a storm of abuse was directed at the nocturnal marauders. They walked down the path quickly and the moon shone bright on the party. Robert was leading the way, Gemma came next and close behind were Caroline and Bianca. It was steep as the path joined the road and Robert gave his hand to each as they climbed down. Then as Robert jumped down after them onto the road there was the report of a pistol or rifle fired very near and a bullet whistled and sang by his ear. At that moment a cloud obscured the moon and they were in darkness. "Run," called Robert and they ran as hard as they could down the road. There was no pursuit and no second shot. When the moon came out, they slowed to a walk, looked at each other breathlessly and laughed.

"Does that often happen here?" asked Caroline. From her voice Robert could tell that she was amused, had not been frightened and had run only because the others ran.

"It wasn't the peasant who had been shouting at us. I saw the flash come from a tree just down the road. There was a man waiting for us there," said Bianca.

"He heard the dog barking and ambushed us. Lucky for Robert that the cloud came over the moon," said Gemma.

179

Robert said nothing. He was very much surprised that he should have been shot at and still more that he should have been shot at so soon — only a few hours after his return to San Frediano. There was no further incident and they walked briskly back to the town. Before parting with Bianca and Emilia at their father's doorstep, Gemma made the girls promise to keep their adventure secret from everyone.

Robert was still far from fit. The midnight cross-country scramble coming after his flight from America and the long drive from the airport to San Frediano on top of his recent illness had left him speechless from exhaustion. He blinked his eyes, walked unsteadily and barely kept control. Gemma was very quiet until they were alone together in the bedroom they were sharing, then she said, "Father must have known you were in great danger! The only words he said when he recovered consciousness were: 'Tell him to take care, to take great care.' It was of this danger that he was thinking. But tell me, honestly, why Angelo wants to have you assassinated? For it was him or one of his men."

"I'm half dead. You know I've been ill. Let's leave it till tomorrow. There's nothing to worry about now," said Robert.

"Father's death has left me with nothing, with almost nothing. I am a broken creature. If you were to be killed owing to my carelessness it would be the end of everything.

He said you must take care and the very first night I lead you out into the night to be murdered by Angelo. But why? Please explain why?"

But Robert was no longer even listening.

"Get into bed. Let's leave it till the morning."

Gemma looked at him with surprise but seeing his hair plastered down, wet with sweat, and the dulled look of exhaustion in his eyes, she got into bed and said no more.

Robert took her in his arms and pressed her body close to his. He had been longing for that moment during the eight weeks of absence. His right arm was round her shoulders and he stretched the hand out to touch her breast; his left hand slid up her thigh . . . and he fell fast asleep.

An hour later he almost woke up and then as he fell into unconsciousness again he was faintly aware of Gemma slipping out of his arms and going out of the bedroom. He roused himself just sufficiently to realize that she was gone and that he was alone; then with the faintest of consolatory reflections: "All's well, why worry?" he fell asleep again.

It was almost midday before he woke up and there was Gemma coming towards him, smiling at him with a bowl of coffee in her hands. He drank it while she sat on the bed.

"How are you now, darling?"

"I'm perfectly all right now. I can't remember quite what happened last night. Why did you go away?"

"You fell asleep just as . . ." Gemma laughed.

Robert took her hand and drew her to him. "Come in here, darling." She shook her head. "Caroline's there, in the next room."

"That doesn't matter." And it did not. An hour later Robert roused himself to look up as Caroline came in. Seeing them lying together in bed her eyes grew hard and bright, the color deepened on her cheeks and she bit her lips before she smiled and spoke.

"You're a disgrace, Gemma. I'm shocked."

Gemma was too sleepy to be immediately responsive; her black mane was tangled, her neck and breast dark gold against the white rose petals of Robert's chest and shoulder. She yawned, blinked, and drew the bedclothes tightly round herself to hide from the scrutiny of the English girl in whose arms she had passed the night.

"Have you told Robert what you decided?" asked Caroline, standing beside the bed. He could see that she was controlling a strong emotion, masking it under a manner of affection and amused detachment.

"Give me a kiss, Caroline," said Robert, watching her closely as he said it. There was a slight glint in her eye, a faint recoil, before she laughed and replied:

"Really, Robert, haven't you any sense of shame, asking for a kiss with Gemma there."

"It's the least you can do if you come walking into our bedroom uninvited. You may give her one too."

The glint of — it was anger — showed again. However, she sat down on the edge of the bed saying, "You're incorrigible. You had better tell him, Gemma."

"Tell me what?" asked Robert. It was a mistake to have asked.

"Oh, Roberto *mio!* Oh, my darling, I have talked it over with Caroline and we have quite decided — it's terrible — but you must go away at once."

"Go away? Where? Why?"

"Your life is in danger. Angelo will have you killed if you stay here."

Robert laughed gently and stroked Gemma's head. Caroline said, "I won't for a moment entertain the idea that Angelo had anything to do with it. For one thing we saw him drive home and he was perfectly friendly to Robert all the evening. But *someone* tried to shoot you last night. You must go away at once."

"Don't be ridiculous. I've come back to marry Gemma."

Caroline's color deepened and she looked at him with very bright eyes.

"You had better both get up now anyway. I'll run the water in the bath and lunch will be ready when you are dressed." When she had gone, Gemma turned and clutched him tightly, kissed him and then looked at him with mournful dark eyes. There were dark circles round them. She was exhausted.

"No, Robert, you must go."

"I'll go anywhere you like, if you'll come too."

"I can't do that at present. I'm tied up with the shop for weeks. And there is the concert tomorrow. I have Michaelis coming as the soloist."

"Well, marry me."

"Perhaps one day. I don't know. There's Caroline."

It was on the tip of Robert's tongue to ask, "What has she got to do with it?" but he restrained himself. It would be better tactics, if Caroline was his rival, or was just making mischief, to give her rope enough, and not to force a show-down. The two women were consulting together about what was to be done about him. He must play it so that Gemma and he would be consulting together on what was to be done about Caroline.

With the idea of compromise, Robert agreed during lunch that he would stay in the house for the rest of that day. Gemma announced that she was going out. Robert said he would take a siesta, for he was still tired after the long flight. But he had hardly lain down on his bed, when Caroline came in, pulled up a chair beside him, and took his hand.

"Robert, my dear, will you let me say what I really feel, what I really think?" Her eyes were very soft and she held his in a long, long look and her lips parted and her breasts rose and fell with her deep breath.

"You don't *belong* here. We *neither* of us belong here.

That is the real reason why you ought to go away; why we *both* ought to go. I don't suppose that you mind having been shot at. You probably think it won't happen again and you may be quite right. You're not in the least bit a coward. But do you understand that it is an appalling strain on Gemma — after her father's death. I'm sure that if you stay here she will break down under the emotional strain. That's why I've decided, after last night, that you *must* go. It's not fair to her, she can't face the idea of another tragedy. I'll fetch your bag from the Salerno woman and drive you into Florence. I've got my car here, you know. If you want me, I'll stay there with you until you are settled in."

Caroline's eyes were large and soft, she smiled, she drew a deep breath and her breasts rose and she leaned over and kissed Robert and then quickly put her hand over his mouth.

"No, don't say anything. It will be quite like old times."

In spite of her words she was waiting for a reply. Robert said nothing.

"That's settled then. I'll make tea now, and I'll tell Gemma when she comes in."

"I don't mind going to Florence with you, so long as we take Gemma with us," said Robert, just before Caroline left the room.

Caroline had gone out before Gemma returned, bringing Robert's bag with her. For a little while they argued inconclusively: Gemma telling Robert that he must leave San Frediano next morning; Robert repeating that he was only too happy to leave if she would come with him.

They had settled nothing when Caroline returned, with her arms full of parcels of food saying that she had met several people and had invited them all to dinner that evening. In Caroline's presence Gemma seemed to shrink into herself and fade. Robert worked with her for the next hour or two in the kitchen helping her while she chopped up garlic and basil, whipped eggs, and threaded pieces of rosemary through the outside of a leg of kid. In the next room Caroline was singing as she laid the table.

The guests, when they came, were not Lucchesi's friends, but a younger generation, few of whom Robert had met, except Bianca and Emilia, though he recognized one young man as Gemma's dancing partner in the Festival of the Grape.

Caroline glowed and sparkled among them, her eyes shining, her laugh ringing, her teeth flashing and her wonderful beauty dominating them all. The three young Italian men preened themselves in her glances; Gemma and the doctor's daughters gazed at her with adoring eyes. Robert sat silent, listening. He heard that the new mayor was to be elected the following week; Angelo was the Communist candidate and was expected to win, though he was violently opposed by the church. The Christian Socialist schoolmaster was not popular.

After dinner they had music and all eyes were upon Caroline as she sat by the piano and sang and one of the young Italians was able to brush her dress with his sleeve as he turned over her music for her when she signaled with a flashing glance.

It was one o'clock in the morning before the visitors had left.

"I shall stay with Caroline tonight," said Gemma in an expressionless voice when he went into what he had called "their bedroom" that morning. She went slowly out of the room. Robert forced himself to lie down but he could not sleep. After a little while, he got out of bed and went to the closed door and listened. There was whispering, then silence. Then he could hear Gemma crying softly:

"Oh! Oh! Oh! . . . Oh! No! Oh! No!" and a gentle laugh from Caroline.

Robert got up early, before either of the girls, made the breakfast and then, leaving the coffee to keep hot on the side of the stove, went out for a walk.

Chapter 12

ALREADY THERE WAS A BREATH OF SPRING IN THE AIR AND THE young corn was just tall enough to ripple in the wind. The sun was hot, the fruit buds swelling and the whole cycle of the year about to start again. In spite of his sleepless night, Robert felt calm and confident as he went over the ground where Gemma had led them on the first night of his return. There was the dog barking furiously, rushing up and down the wire beside the path, there the man who had cursed them planting cabbages in the manured field, there chickens running to and fro, and the path dipping sharply to the high road. There was the point where he had jumped down on the road — and there, only twelve yards away, was a plane tree from behind which Angelo must have shot at him. The ground below was too stony and hard for footprints, but there probably, would be the ejected cartridge case in the ditch. It took Robert nearly a quarter of an hour before he found it: a clean little .38 brass shell.

Robert put it into his pocket and walked back to the town. It was past ten o'clock by the time he had reached the palace and had rung Angelo's bell. There were big notices of the piano recital at which Michaelis would be playing that afternoon.

An old woman opened the door and he waited while she fetched her master.

"Do you mind if I come in? I want to talk to you."

"Sure, Mr. Harcourt."

Robert walked first and Angelo followed him into the office. They sat down.

"Like some whisky?"

"Too early in the morning for me."

"And me too. Well, what ya got to tell me?" said Angelo gravely.

"I want to tell you all about what I did when I was in America and why I did it."

"I would certainly like to hear that," said Angelo.

"When I went back, I took with me a complete set of your fingerprints and several good photographs. The F.B.I. have nothing on you, but the day I left I turned them in to the Military Police, together with your present address and occupations and everything that Lucchesi had been able to find out about you."

Angelo sat perfectly still. He looked like an idol. Not even his eyes moved. After a short silence Robert went on, "I don't know whether they've anything against you or not; they probably would not care to tell me. But you will know. Maybe they are still looking through their files. If you aren't in the records, they can't do anything. If they have you in the files and they think you are a big enough fish to make it worth while, they'll catch up on you."

Angelo moistened his lips with a quick tongue but said nothing.

Robert continued, still speaking slowly, "You can shoot me full of holes if you want to. But it won't help you any. One more killing will just make the record worse."

"Why d'ya come tell me this?"

"One or two reasons. First I want you to lay off shooting at me. It can't do you any good, even if you hit me next time. It may do you quite a lot of harm."

"When did I ever shoot at you?"

"Two nights ago. You knew I was going for that midnight walk. No one else did and the man who fired was waiting for me to come out on the road. I think you have got a .38 pistol." Robert took the empty brass cartridge case out of his pocket and handed it to Angelo, who looked at it, smiled and put it on the table.

"What's given you the notion that I'm an American citizen? Do I look and act more like a Yank than any other Italian who has been in the States?"

"No. You don't really. My folks live up in Vermont. I've

never lived in Syracuse or Brooklyn. So I'm not an expert."

"Well, then?"

"It was old Bannerman. He took for granted that you were an American, then I began to imagine I saw little touches. Lucchesi thought it very suspicious the way you faded out when the American Army took over from the British."

"That was years back, during the war."

"Your fingerprints haven't changed and the record will be in the files."

"I think you are nuts. Coming here and telling me you've been fingerprinting me, going to the States to try and ruin me. Don't you think I might be sore at you?"

"I think you probably are sore. But you have a cool head and a long head, Angelo."

"What was the other reason for coming here? You said there was two."

"Well. I can't be sure. But you shot at me from only twelve yards away in bright moonlight and if you are the sort of man I think, you wouldn't have missed. And though I believe you killed Lucchesi I don't think you would choose to shoot me with those girls there. You could get me alone any time."

An indescribably sly look came over Angelo's face as Robert spoke.

"But you ain't scared?"

"No. I'm not. But Gemma is."

"You reckon to marry that girl, if you live long enough?"

"I shall, if I can get rid of Caroline Stephenson."

"It was she asked me to take that crack at you. You heard her tip me off."

For a moment both men thought about Caroline. Then Angelo said, "Lucchesi and you thought to stop me running for mayor by digging out the dirt?"

"Yes."

"And you think you still can?"

"I wasn't thinking about that at all. I just want you to lay off shooting at me. If you are an American with a criminal record they'll get you whether you are mayor or whether you're not. If you haven't a record and aren't an American citizen, you're safe. I can't do anything more. Either way it's a waste of time to shoot at me — especially if you don't want to hit."

"Ya. You've told me that twice. Anything else you want to say?"

"I came up here partly because if you only want to scare me I thought I would give you a warning. There's time enough for you to clear out before they come for you."

"Quite an idea, and thanks a lot for coming in." They stood up and Angelo accompanied him to the door.

"Well, son. I won't shoot again except to kill. I never

touched Lucchesi. It sure shook me when I learned that he had bought it. And give my love to that lovely limey."

Robert walked back into the little town. It was market day; the booths filled the piazza with their canvas roofs and walls, pitched against the arcades. The noise of the market women and cheapjacks rose like the clamor of birds on a spring morning in England: rooks cawing, thrushes and blackbirds singing, starlings whistling. One canvas street was filled with rolls of gaily printed cottons, ready-made clothes and women's shoes; nearby, the cheesemonger was weighing out fragments split off from his huge black Parmesan cheeses, flanked by the smaller millstones of Pecorino. Next to him the fishmonger was standing behind his boxes of red mullets and young octopuses and cutting an almost purple steak off half an immense tunny — all fresh from Cesenatico. There was a booth selling nothing but oil and one with huge demijohns of San Giovese wine. And round the corner were the butchers, poulterers and pork butchers, and then booths selling spring vegetables forced in Sicily and Calabria, and a florist with carnations grown under glass, from Pescia.

Robert began buying food. He thought that he would like to come back with his arms full of gifts. He imagined Gemma's pleasure as he spread them out in the kitchen. There would be time enough to cook a guinea fowl stuffed with chestnuts, trussed and ready for roasting. He bought also a whole kilo of early asparagus, half a dozen eggs and a two-liter flash of Broglio Chianti so that for once they could have a good red wine. He could carry no more, and with these he went back to the shop and as there was no answer to the bell, he let himself in by the side door with the key Gemma had given him months ago — before he went to America.

The flat was empty. Robert took his purchases into the kitchen. He smeared the bird with oil, pinned two slices of bacon over the breast and put it in the oven. Then he put salted water on to boil for the asparagus. While it was heating he washed up the breakfast cups and plates. It was delightful to steal a march on Gemma — to have the lunch cooking and the flat tidy before she came back and to be able to show her that he bore her no ill will for having been seduced by Caroline the previous night. He could show her that he wasn't jealous — which Caroline could never do. Gemma would feel gratitude and her mood would respond to the love shown in his preparations. Indeed, while he rushed around the kitchen he felt no jealousy and none of the unhappy resentment which had kept him awake during the night.

While the asparagus was cooking, Robert made a thick mayonnaise sauce, stopping to baste the guinea fowl and lower the flame of the oven. Then he drained the lovely symbolic stalks and spread them out on a big dish on the window sill to cool. He laid the table and then saw that something else would be needed — he would go out and buy a salad to go with the bird, and flowers for the table. Why, he wondered, were the girls out for so long? Perhaps they had gone up to the dance hall to get it ready for the concert. When he reached the piazza, the market people were already packing up their booths. The crisp lettuces were all gone and so had the delicious curly endive, but he managed to find some of the oak-leaved lettuce with no heart. Then with a dozen red and white carnations he went back.

He unlocked the door and went up, but as he opened the door of the flat, Gemma rushed up to him and pushed him back and then stepped out on to the landing and pulled the door shut behind her. He had never seen her look like that before.

"What are you doing here? I've told you that you must go away. Can't you understand? I don't want you here! No, I won't let you come in! The room is full of people; there's Michaelis, and Caroline's asked everybody she can think of. Angelo may be here in a minute."

Robert stared at her petrified, but still without comprehension and mechanically gave her the sheaf of flowers and the bag of lettuce, and Gemma unclenched her tight fists to take them. Her face was pale and her mouth working. Robert thought that she looked like a serpent.

"Oh! Please, please, go away! Go away to Florence, or anywhere. I can't have you here. You can't stay here. Surely you can see that!"

"I think you are very unkind. I never expected you to be so unkind," said Robert.

"I don't like feebleness and kind, feeble people," said Gemma, hissing the words and pushing the door open with her elbow, she stepped back into the room and shut it in his face. Robert walked down into the street. Everything was unreal. What in God's name did she mean by feebleness? Scarcely aware of what he was doing, Robert went into the shop and said to the young manager whom he had met for the first time two nights before, "Would you be so kind as to go upstairs and tell the Signorina Gemma that I left a guinea fowl in the oven?"

The young man stared at him in surprise and said, "Certainly. A guinea fowl. I shall be delighted." Then he added from habit, "Is there anything else you will be wanting, Sir?"

Robert shook his head and walked out. In the piazza the last booths were being loaded onto trucks. He sat down and ordered a Stock brandy. But when the waiter had poured it out, Robert found that his hand was shaking so badly that he spilled most of it.

> " 'And is thy heart so strong
>   As for to leave me thus?' "

he said aloud, remembering that he had sent Gemma an
edition of Wyatt's poems from New York. Her heart must
be strong because she didn't like feebleness. How did that
other poem go?

> " 'I promised you,
>   And you promised me,
>   To be as true
>   As I would be.
>   But since I see
>   Your double heart,
>   Farewell my part!' "

"Is it possible? Yes, all is possible."

Robert was drinking his third glass of Stock and the feeling of shock was giving way to a dull anger and resentment,
when a hand suddenly descended on his shoulder and looking round he saw to his horror the smiling face of Ercole
Beccofilandria.

"I've been looking for you all over the town. Thank goodness, I've found you. I was told you were probably on the
bus for Forlì. I've a surprise for you, my dearest American
friend." And without being invited, Ercole flung himself
into the chair opposite, and grinning from ear to ear,
counted out six ten-thousand lire notes.

"What on earth . . ." began Robert.

"Here is the money you sent me. It saved my life. And, now, would you believe it? I've fallen on my feet. I'm a reformed character."

"What's happened to you?" asked Robert, thinking that he must be feeble if he couldn't shake off Ercole. However, he gathered up the notes.

"I've just got married. I'm wildly happy. My wife is the widow of a bookseller in Bologna. I love the work. I can tell you there's nothing like innocence! Love! Springtime! Our shop is an oasis in the desert.

"I read the divine Tasso aloud to Rebecca, only interrupting myself to put notes for a thousand lires into the till every half-hour. Do you know that I believe in humanity — except yesterday, when I caught a nun stealing a torn copy of Moravia's *A Woman of Rome* out of the two-hundred lire box!" Ercole burst out laughing, but then suddenly asked, "But what's the matter, old friend? You're shivering. Aren't you well?"

"Nothing to matter," said Robert.

"It's cold here. Come indoors and have lunch with me. You'll feel a different man when you've eaten. I thought Signorina Gemma looked like death warmed up when I asked for you five minutes ago. Don't tell me all about it. You'll be sure to regret it if you do."

Robert followed Ercole into the restaurant upstairs, noticing that they attracted some curious glances. Soon he had stopped shivering and could smile at Ercole's stories. An hour and a half later he was a different man. He had eaten a huge meal of lasagne and of roast kid, and had drunk almost a liter of Chianti. By the time they were sipping the little cups of *espresso* coffee, he had decided that he would not submit tamely to such treatment. He would see Gemma that night and have it out with Caroline.

Ercole might be an unmitigated scoundrel but he did not ask Robert a single word about what had upset him, or about his private affairs. Instead of that he kept up a stream of amusing stories and insisted on paying the bill.

Finally he said, "I shall have to be tootling off on my Vespa, soon. My wife doesn't like me riding on the Via Emilia after dark."

"You won't come to the concert with me?" asked Robert.

"No fear. I only came here today to see my stepmother and in the hopes of finding you."

Robert watched the little man straddle his motor scooter and set off. Then he walked slowly up to the palace. There was a big station wagon in the inner courtyard and Signora Angelo came out carrying a typewriter and put it in the back. It was loaded with office files and steel boxes. From the first floor came the sound of the piano. The Russian woman caught sight of Robert and he saw her draw a deep breath as though she were going to shout at him. Then she went back into the building. Robert ran quickly up the marble stairs and rang the bell of the bishop's apartments. A man-servant opened the door, smiled at Robert and said, "My Lord has been expecting you. He is very weak. You must not stay more than a few minutes." Robert followed him and found himself being shown into the great state bed-room with the frescoes of Diana and her companions, armed with boar spears on the wall opposite the great green and gilt bed in which the bishop was lying between a very coarsely woven pair of homespun linen sheets. He was wear-ing a white linen nightshirt drawn tight round his neck with a string and a white linen nightcap on his head, the tassel of which fell forward over his forehead. With his big nutcracker nose and protruding lower jaw he looked exactly like a querulous sick Punchinello.

From below, the crashing chords of Beethoven could be heard. The bishop smiled and spoke, but his voice was so weak that Robert realized that he was very near to death.

"For the first time I feel grateful to you and Signorina Lucchesi — and of course your friend Angelo. I've been en-joying the music so much."

"I believe that we shall soon be rid of him," said Robert.

"Rid of whom?" asked the old man with a sudden fierce look.

"Unless I'm much mistaken, he will be gone tomorrow,"

replied Robert. "If I am right you ought to be sure to seize the lower floors of the palace immediately, in case he tries to sublet them to anyone."

The old face flushed in excitement and there was something like a sparkle in the tired sunken eyes.

"I thought for the first moment you meant that you would soon be rid of me. But do you mean Angelo?"

Robert nodded his head.

"If I can live until he has gone! Is it your doing?" he asked, interrupting himself.

"I warned him this morning that he might be in danger if he stayed. Now I think he is going."

"You have relieved me of the burden of guilt. I shall not be afraid to die now," said the bishop, and Robert realized suddenly that the old man had been afraid of death precisely because he felt that he had betrayed his trust.

"And the election is in two days' time," whispered the bishop.

The manservant entered the room, bowed to Robert and said, "Signore, you must come now."

The old man held out a withered claw over the rough sheet and Robert noticed the big pastoral ring. He lifted the hand and was about to kiss the ring, when the old man turned the old brown hand dotted with brown spots, palm uppermost. Robert kissed the palm with a feeling of deep tenderness.

"Do you know why I turned my hand over?" asked the bishop, smiling.

Robert shook his head.

"Because I think you like me as a man and not because I am a bishop, and that's how I want it."

"I sure do," said Robert.

From the palace he walked back into the town and let himself into the empty flat. He had eaten and drunk too much with Ercole and felt absolutely exhausted. He must rest. First, however, he collected his possessions and put them in his bag. His red silk pajamas were not on the bed, not under the pillow, or in any of the drawers. They had vanished. One of the girls must have hidden them.

In the dining room the chairs were pushed back from the table and there were dirty plates with cigarette ends and ash clinging to the butter. In the kitchen were piled dirty plates and dishes. All the food he had prepared had been eaten and the flask of wine was empty. There had been eight people to lunch; two men and six women to judge by the lipstick on the cigarette butts on the plates.

Robert lay down on the bed, and in a few minutes was asleep. An hour later he woke up, feeling refreshed. The concert would be over; the girls would be coming back, possibly bringing Michaelis with them. He went out and bought a bottle of French brandy saying to himself, "Damn the expense! I don't like Stock, and *grappa* is rot-gut!"

Then going back to the café he ordered an *espresso* and taking a piece of paper out of his pocket he wrote:

An Analysis:
Only by exercising power can Caroline permit herself physical love. Otherwise she would not respect herself.

Gemma was in love with Caroline as a child before she ever met Robert.

Robert was given passionate love, but was maltreated because he refused to accept Gemma's judgment.

Contrariwise, Robert took advantage of Gemma, whose physical passions are very strong, and tried to impose himself and change her way of life. He therefore deserved what he got.

After a time he got up and went down to the movie in the bottom of the town. It was almost empty and the few girls who were there seemed to look at him oddly and took seats in other rows.

Chapter 13

WHEN ROBERT CAME IN THE TWO GIRLS WERE IN THE KITCHEN, Caroline washing and Gemma drying. Gemma gave him an imploring look, asking for forgiveness or begging him not to start an emotional scene. He was not sure which.

"Have some brandy?" he said, and poured out three large tots.

"I don't think I want any," said Caroline, wrinkling her nose.

"O.K.," and Robert poured the glass he had intended for her into his own. Gemma accepted the one he gave her, drank a gulp and said, "Thank you very much, Robert. That's just what I needed."

He cut himself two slices of bread, buttered them and made himself a salami sandwich. They none of them spoke while he was eating.

"I don't like weaklings any more than you do, Gemma," said Robert.

"Is that remark personal?" asked Caroline in a clear, rather strained voice.

"Yes, but nobody thinks you're a weakling, Caroline," said Robert.

"Oh, must you go into this?" said Gemma.

"If you had told me earlier — or if you had left a note when you went out, explaining that you would prefer me to have lunch out, because of the concert, you would have saved me a very great deal of pain."

"It isn't for you to talk of being inconsiderate," said Caroline. "You refuse to leave the town, although Gemma continually begs you to do so and you know that she is very much alarmed thinking that somebody or other is going to shoot you and she will feel responsible. I could not care less, if you were shot, except on Gemma's account."

"Is that the only reason that you want me to go away?" he asked.

Gemma went up to him where he was sitting and took his hand and stroked it. She looked at him with lackluster eyes.

"It's such a strain," she said in a low voice.

"I'm not in the slightest danger and don't think that I have been," said Robert. He drank a mouthful of brandy and began telling them about his visit to Angelo that morning, but was interrupted two or three times by Gemma exclaiming: "You didn't!" and then: "You must have been mad!" and then: "That's the bravest thing I've ever heard of! I don't think even my father would have done that! And you were unarmed!"

"It wasn't brave at all. Angelo is a very intelligent man. He only shot at me to scare me into leaving the town. Caroline put him up to it, or asked him to."

Gemma turned and the two girls looked at each other.

"I suppose you think that I ought to apologize," said Caroline.

"But really . . ." She left her sentence unfinished.

"I think you have behaved abominably to Robert and I have been very unjust," said Gemma. "And you have behaved most treacherously to me — persuading me to drive Robert away because I thought he was in danger of his life . . . How could you?"

"Have some more brandy?" said Robert. Gemma shook her head and Robert slopped some more into his glass.

"I'm going to bed now. Promise to come to my room when you are ready."

He turned in the open doorway and looked back at the girls. Gemma was facing him; she looked very unhappy; tears were not far away. Behind her stood Caroline, tall, and upright. Robert thought he had never seen her look more beautiful — her head was thrown a little back, her lips parted, her color was high and her whole expression and the bearing of her body defiant.

Gemma nodded her head and made a slight movement towards him, but Caroline put her hand on her shoulder and held her back.

"You are insufferably possessive, Robert," said Caroline.

He pushed open his bedroom door, and carrying his glass of brandy carefully, went out and shut it behind him. Then, when he had taken off his coat and trousers, he went back in his shirt and trunks and asked:

"What's happened to my pajamas?"

The girls looked at him, they were still standing in the same position. Gemma's whole expression changed; she started forward and gave a rather embarrassed laugh. Then, going into the other bedroom, she came back with them. There was a slight blush on her cheek.

"Yes, Robert. I'll come in a little while," she said in a low voice as she tossed them to him. Robert shut his door, finished undressing, got into bed and switched out the light.

Gemma did not come. After two hours, Robert switched on his light, and looked at his watch. It was two o'clock in the morning. He finished the drop of brandy in his glass, got out of bed and went to listen at the door of the girls' room. Caroline was talking, explaining something.

Robert opened the door and turned on the light. Gemma was lying on her back, Caroline on the far side of the bed had an arm round her neck, holding her. Robert sat down on the edge of the bed by Gemma's knees.

"Why didn't you come?" he asked.

"She changed her mind," said Caroline angrily.

"You must see the whole situation is impossible; the strain is too great," said Gemma.

"You are drunk, Robert. You simply stink of brandy. Pull yourself together and go back to bed," said Caroline.

"You loved me when we were in Florence; I think that you still love me," said Robert. "All the time that I was away in America I was longing for you, expecting to marry you when I got back. Do you really want Caroline to ruin our lives?"

"Gemma can see that you are much too possessive — and like most Americans, you are a drunk," said Caroline. "I've told you all about him, Gemma. Better learn by my experience than have to find out for yourself."

Robert paid no attention to these words and began speaking as though he and Gemma had been alone together.

"I know how you feel about her; I understand your being seduced by her, because I have been in love with her fatal beauty myself. And I know what you felt about her when you were a child. But what I don't understand is how you let her persuade you to be so abominably unkind to me this morning. How could you have turned me out of the house suddenly, without a word of warning, when I was coming back with my hands full of flowers for you? How could you

have allowed yourself to be so devilishly cruel? Lying in bed
I have been repeating to myself:

> 'And wilt thou leave me thus,
> That hath given thee my heart
> Never for to depart
> Neither for pain nor smart:
> And wilt thou leave me thus?
> Say nay! Say nay!'

Is it possible? What have I done to deserve such treatment? What can I do? What can I do?"

Robert stopped. His voice was breaking and he was shivering violently.

"Don't say any more. You are shivering. You'll get pneumonia again. You can't sleep, I don't suppose any of us will
sleep. You had better get into bed with us," said Gemma.

"This is really fantastic," said Caroline angrily, as Gemma
made room and Robert squeezed into the bed. She still had
Gemma by the shoulders but she suddenly began laughing.

"It is far more like Opera Buffo than like Casanova's
memoirs," said Robert, and at this Gemma began to laugh
also, and freeing herself from Caroline's clutch she switched
out the light.

"Not that I should really mind if you did behave like
Casanova," she said, turning towards Robert.

After a little while he asked, "What had you done with my pajamas?"

"I hid them. I wanted to have something of yours if you went away," she replied.

"I won't stay here to listen to such maudlin sentimentality! Why should I care what happens to you, you baby!" exclaimed Caroline. But Robert was already kissing Gemma and as Caroline scrambled across them and jumped off the bed, his kiss was returned. The door slammed and they were alone, but it no longer mattered much to them whether they were alone or not.

Robert and Gemma clung to each other seeking not pleasure, not satisfaction, not to enjoy or to be enjoyed, but with a desperate frenzy to be reconciled, to belong to one another, to be part of each other. Love ran its course and at last they came both together and when the extremity of passion had spent itself in each, they lay motionless in a profound peace, in a calm of the spirit that it seemed nothing could disturb. But before they slept Robert said, "Let us leave here and go to stay with Giovanna in the morning."

"That would be the best thing we could do," replied Gemma.

Robert was careful not to say that Giovanna thought Caroline was evil. He did not believe in making moral judgments — he did not really think anyone was evil. But Caroline would not follow them up the mountain. He fell asleep.

The all-night bell that Lucchesi had fixed on the wall over his bed, in case a prescription was urgently needed during the night, began ringing steadily.

"It must be someone wanting the shop," said Gemma. "It's four in the morning," she added, after she had switched on the light. Robert had come to, from a long way off. "I will go and tell them where to find the manager." She got out of bed and Robert, only waiting to find and to put on his pajamas, followed her out of the room, to the head of the stairs. He was not going to run any risk of losing Gemma again in Caroline's bed. There was a gabble in Italian patois at the street door, and then Gemma called up the stairs, "It's the Signora Bannerman. There's been an accident and she wants you, Robert. It sounds a bit odd." She came back, leaving the street door open.

"Well, I had better go. Will you come along with me, Gemma?"

Robert put on his trousers and pulled his shirt over his head.

"Of course I'll come with you. Take my father's pistol. It might be some kind of a trap," said Gemma, clipping her skirt and pulling on a jersey.

"No. I shan't want that. But bring a torch. Did she say what it was?"

"No, only that it was something terrible."

They tiptoed through the rooms and down the stairs to avoid having to explain to Caroline what had happened. The light in her room was on. They could hear her moving, but she did not speak. It was long before dawn and there was no moon, but the starlight was so bright that there was almost enough light to see their way. Robert and Gemma walked very fast to keep up with the old woman trotting at their side. The little circle of light from the electric torch often fell on her bare ankles and calves, which were well-shaped and muscular as a girl's.

"What's wrong?" Robert asked her once.

"Terrible. Terrible. You'll see; we're nearly there," she replied.

The iron gate was unlocked and ajar, but when they had gone down the avenue the house door was locked and they waited while Signora Bannerman fished up a huge iron door-key from between her breasts and slipped the string over her head. She led them through a dark hall into a small room which was brilliantly lit up. Angelo was sitting on the floor with his legs stretched straight in front of him and his back propped against the front of an old steel safe, the thick door of which swung open drunkenly. Several packets of ten-thousand lire notes had tumbled out onto the floor. There were some tools and some kind of blowtorch. Behind the table old Mr. Bannerman sat with his head buried in his hands. He did not look up and for a moment Robert wondered if there was anything the matter with him. Looking closer, he could see that he was all right. But Angelo's face was the color of dirty wax and was streaming with sweat. Even his hair was wet; his lips, fingers and nails were all bloodless, like dead worms. Robert guessed that he was bleeding to death from an internal wound and that it would be dangerous to move him. He dropped on his knees to feel his pulse. There was fear in Angelo's eyes and he whispered, "The priest." Old Bannerman had looked up.

"What's he saying now?" he asked.

"He's asking for a priest," Robert shouted in his ear.

"Oh, aye. I would never allow one of them into the house —but we must indulge the poor rascal in his superstition." The old man's words were harsh, but his voice was not far from tears.

"Gimme a cigarette," whispered Angelo. Robert pulled out a pack of Chesterfields, lit one, and put it in Angelo's mouth. A faint twitch at the corners of the bloodless lips indicated gratitude.

He pulled once or twice feebly and blew a whiff of smoke from his nostrils. He gazed at Gemma with very bright eyes and tried to speak but without success. Sweat dripped from his nose, ran down his upper lip and soaked through an inch of the cigarette butt.

"He ought to be kept warm. I'll fill some bottles with hot

water," said Gemma and went out of the room followed by the old woman. The three men were alone. Angelo's eyes were fixed on Robert and he made a faint beckoning gesture with his head. The cigarette fell. Robert knelt beside the dying man and Angelo breathed rather than spoke the words "I swear I never knocked off Lucchesi. Don't let her think I did."

The next moment there was the crunch of tires and the sound of arrivals.

A small boy in a white cassock came into the room tinkling a little bell and Father Anselmo and the doctor came in.

"He's dying from an internal hemorrhage," said the doctor. "You can do more for him than I can."

The priest bent over Angelo and there was the low singsong of Latin words and a touching of the lips with the Eucharist and marking a cross on the forehead with the holy oil. But looking at Angelo's face Robert could see that he was already dead, and when Gemma came in with three whisky bottles filled with hot water to prop round him, there was no longer any doubt of it. Robert looked at the priest, remembering that he was also an initiate of the Dianic cult.

Then two *carabinieri* came into the room, followed by an officer, and after a little while Angelo's body was put onto a stretcher and removed. The doctor and the priest with his acolyte drove away, but Robert and Gemma waited while old Bannerman answered questions which Robert translated and shouted into his ear.

The old man always slept badly and was accustomed to wander round the house in the early hours; that morning he had found Angelo on his knees in front of the safe. Angelo had reached for his pistol and Bannerman had shot him through the chest. At first the police seemed to find the story incredible. The Signor Angelo was running for mayor! But a messenger who had been sent to the palace to fetch his wife, returned with the news that she had left the previous evening driving a heavily laden car. The Angelos' rooms in the palace were deserted and most of their portable possessions were gone. Angelo must have intended to rejoin her when he had cracked the safe.

A policeman picked up the packets of notes lying on the floor which nobody had touched and put them back in the safe and propped the door shut with a poker. Signora Bannerman brought in a tray of coffee and hot milk and they stood round in desultory fashion trying to think of subjects for conversation, but every remark fell flat. Suddenly old Bannerman drank off his cup of coffee and stood up. His blue eyes were bloodshot, his long white hair tangled, his big hands trembled, but in spite of his drunkard's look, there was majesty in the man.

"All my fault!" he said in a loud voice. "Lucchesi told me

what would happen! I have never killed a man before! I shan't forgive myself."

Trembling and staggering, he began to leave the room and his old wife ran to take his arm.

Outside the sun had just risen; a warbler was singing a pretty song over and over again in the acacias; an armed policeman keeping guard over Angelo's black V-8 at the gateway, nodded to them. The big car was loaded with bags and boxes.

Robert and Gemma walked slowly back towards the little town with their long shadows dancing before them over the uneven track. In one of the fields a peasant was leading out his yoke of white oxen to harness to the plough; there were women hoeing under the vines. Matins were over and the little town seemed deserted. They did not meet anyone as they crossed the piazza, and when they went upstairs into the flat they found that it was empty and that they were alone.

An hour later they had packed all they would need in a rucksack and were on their way up the winding goat track that led into the high mountains. They would stay with Giovanna for the week before their marriage.

THE END